DEAD DROP

F. C. Malby

Published by Linen Press, London 2022
8 Maltings Lodge
Corney Reach Way
London W4 2TT
www.linen-press.com

This book is a work of fiction. All the characters, incidents, events, organisations, and places portrayed in these pages are either drawn from the author's imagination or are used fictitiously. Any resemblance to actual persons, living or dead, is entirely coincidental. Readers are requested to bear in mind that portrayal of any kind of dialogue, opinion, view, subject, habit or character trait may not necessarily be the standpoint of the author or the publisher and does not in any way imply advocacy.

A CIP catalogue record for this book is available from the British Library.

Cover art: Arcangel
Cover Design: Lynn Michell
Typeset by Zebedee
Printed and bound by Lightning Source
ISBN: 978-1-9196248-6-0

About the Author

Author photograph by Diana Moschitz

F. C. Malby graduated with a first-class joint honours degree in Geography and Education. She has travelled widely and spent eight years living in Central Europe. She worked as a photographer and a teacher, teaching English in the Czech Republic, in Badjao communities in the Philippines and in London. She writes novels, short stories and poetry. Her debut novel, *Take Me to the Castle*, set in the Czech Republic, won The People's Prize. Her debut short story collection, *My Brother Was a Kangaroo*, includes award-winning stories, many of which have been published in literary journals and magazines worldwide. She is a contributor to several anthologies, including *In Defence of Pseudoscience: Reflex Fiction Volume Five* (Reflex Press), *Unthology 8* (Unthank Books), and *Hearing Voices: The Litro Anthology of New Fiction* (Kingston University Press) alongside Pulitzer prize winner, Anthony Doerr.

PRAISE FOR F. C. MALBY'S WRITING

PRAISE FOR DEAD DROP

'An exquisitely written, poetic journey through the underbelly of Vienna's artworld is littered with secrets and laced with tension.'
– Jane Isaac

'A lyrical, daring thriller that hurls you into the dark world of art theft with unexpected insights.'
– Stephanie Carty, author of *Shattered*

'Malby's novel proves once and for all that thrillers can be both hugely compelling and beautifully written. This is virtuosic storytelling, as vibrant as a Klimt painting, as lyrical as a Viennese waltz, as atmospheric as a Carol Reed film. I loved it.'
– Jonathan P Taylor, author and Senior Lecturer in Creative Writing, University of Leicester

MY BROTHER WAS A KANGAROO AND OTHER STORIES

'The stories will resonate with you long after finishing.'
– Avril Joy, Costa Short Story Award winner

'F. C. Malby is one of those writers who makes you sit up and pay attention. She's a natural storyteller, a gifted wordsmith, and fearless in taking her imagination to the dark side when the story requires it.'
– Dan Coxon, Fiction Editor, Litro Magazine

'Malby's writing is restrained, understated and elegant. Her shorter fiction pieces are stunning, creating a sense of beauty and poignancy in just a few hundred words.'
– Maureen Scott, CEO, Ether Books

'Deeply moving and attuned to the subtleties of human relationships, F. C. Malby's stories make us realise we're only one step away from a completely different world.'
– Ashley Stokes, Editorial Director, Unthank Books

'F. C. Malby's short story collection is a sensual experience. She has the ability to create scenarios, using sights, smells and sounds which transport the reader straight into the depths of her worlds ... Malby has a knack for capturing salient moments and bringing them to sumptuous life.'
– Shirley Golden, Editor, Flash Flood Journal

Readers' Reviews

TAKE ME TO THE CASTLE

'Such a wonderfully addictive book with beautiful characterisation and imagery. You really feel like you are watching history unfold – so well written. I cannot wait to read F. C. Malby's next book – certainly an author on my 'must read list!'

'Malby navigates these difficult waters with ease and you are transported into not only an emotional quagmire, but a moral one as people make life decisions that have far reaching effects on the lives of others. Brilliantly done.'

'Lovely portrayal of people dealing with massive national and personal change in Eastern Europe. Well researched and clear, but most of all her characters are extremely real and believable. Difficult to put down at times and I keep thinking about the characters, even now! Great insight into the human condition and subtlety shown in her writing. Get it and read it!'

'This book is "un-put-down-ably good" which from me is the highest accolade I can offer! Only a few amazing stories like "Eyes of the Dragon," by Stephen King, and "Captain Corelli's Mandolin" have had me similarly engrossed enough for a single-day read through. Take Me to the Castle has a wonderful pace. Malby masterfully draws you in deeper to their world and their lives; like slowly peeling layers off to reveal a masterpiece. You find yourself building connection and empathy with every page turn.'

THE BENCH

'This is minimalist writing at its best.'

'A compelling yet quietly unsettling short story of expectations, loss and memories.'

BIRD

'What an exquisitely beautifully told story. It's a treasure, pure poetry.'

'I rarely give any writer five stars, but this story deserves them all.'

For Toyin, my fellow traveller on this writing journey

Chapter 1

I hear the roll and clunk of the train's wheels on the steel tracks below, feel its vibrations in my toes and through my thighs as it leaves the platform. The wind rushes into the tunnel from Stephansplatz, its caress warm as it whips down the steps to the underground platform and fills the void.

The Vienna spring brings with it cherry blossom and azure skies, the blues becoming celestial in the late afternoon light. Most count the short, hot summer months. I count the winter months until spring, and then when the leaves turn to a deep, burnt amber, I begin again.

As I reach the top step, a body lies on the pavement, feet contorted, laces undone, socks pushing through holes in the soles. A red, woollen hat rests on the concrete slab by his head, hands clutch an empty bottle of Kaiser beer. Not a soul stops to look. A body littering the pavement is a familiar sight on this part of the underground. It's not always clear whether the person is alive or dead.

I am here for the note. Stepping closer to avoid the people coming up the steps behind me, I spot a corner of paper in his top jacket pocket and pull it free. Without reading the words, I slide it into my jacket. Checking the pocket on the other side of his jacket, I feel something hard and rough and pull out a brooch shaped like a star. I count the spokes, ten of them, and run my fingers across its surface. It lacks the pearls, but at a guess it would have been handcrafted by Hapsburg jeweller, Rozet und Fischmeister. I slip it into my pocket. An unexpected treasure. Reaching down and taking his wrist, I feel for a pulse. I should have checked it first but this is new territory for me. All signs of life have drained away and death was recent. A touch of heat still lingers on the skin, rough and calloused. I pull the hat down over his face. The beer bottle, I suspect, will have been planted to make this look like a natural event. He should have been alive when I reached him.

I stride across the concrete slabs towards the front door of the cathedral. The façade is a gothic foray of limestone circles, arches and towers, the outer layers charred with the fires of change. Digging my gloved fingers deep into the right hand pocket of my coat, I feel the star brooch as it clinks against a few loose coins. I lift them out and slip them into my left pocket before entering the cathedral. I pull each fingertip of the gloves and slide them off my hands. It's too warm to be wearing gloves at this time of year. I touch the stone arch as I enter the building, feel history seep through my fingertips, and pass through the interior door, leaving the light behind. I feel the weight of the wood panelling as it swings back towards my body.

It takes a few moments for my eyes to adjust to the darkness. My lungs fill with incense. I think of priests preparing for sacrament, imagine the scent of purification infusing the chambers of the cathedral, prayers rising upwards.

Omama brought me here when I was six years old. It was beautiful, haunting, like the Grimm's fairy tales she used to read. I arrive for prayer each morning before work. It fills a gap in the empty spaces of my days, and sometimes, my soul. Morning Mass is in progress. I turn right and go into the side chapel to pray. It wouldn't be right to sit through Mass, not now. I gave up using rosary beads a long time ago and don't genuflect when I reach the statue of Mary. I'm alone when I enter the chapel, leaving behind the tourists circling the area at the back, gazing up at the organ pipes and looking through the stained glass window. Others are part of the congregation closer to the front. Some are down on bended knee, demonstrating a reverence I wish I shared.

Judgement can be crippling, but here in the sanctuary I feel a rare acceptance. Echoes of a hymn hang in the silence of St. Eligius's Chapel and a shaft of light pierces the high window and falls on the altar dedicated to St. Valentine. Fresh flowers have been arranged to the right and the nectar gives off a sweet scent. I kneel down with my left hand in my pocket, check the position of the star, and close my eyes. I confess to my theft, glance at my watch and rise from my knees. Tomorrow is a new day, Omama used to say, but I always manage to tarnish it: a harsh word, an unsavoury thought, a brooch slipped into my pocket. I walk towards the flowers and pick a single bloom, twirl it between my fingers, and leave the building.

The smell of fresh espresso from Café Aida mingles with the scent of spring. The corner rooms of converted rooftops rise above the turrets and spires, reminding me of glasshouses and art studios. The copper-roofed domes have turned a marine shade of grey-green, the metals oxidised by humid air - a natural artist at work.

I turn left down Kärntner Straße, passing Swarovski and designer jewellery shops, guards standing a metre from each entrance. The windows of Café Gerstner are filled with miniature pralines and pink macaroons, waiting to be chosen and packed up in mint green boxes with gold-swirled lettering and the Gerstner crest: a coat of arms for the keeper of deer, its origins found in the Yiddish name Hirsh from the blessing of Jacob to his sons. A name is important, so, too, are its origins. High on the wall to the right at Number 16 is a mural detailed in gold leaf of several figures who watch people pass on the street below. It's too high for most to notice, but I notice. I turn left and push through the glass door of Café Heiner, clutching the gold handle. I smile at Ulrike, who is wrapping individual slices of *Nusstorte* and *Sachertorte* for a customer. I could encase these slices in my sleep – remember each tuck and fold, and where the sticker is positioned to seal the cellophane packaging – and construct the boxes blindfolded. Any action repeated over and over becomes completely automatic like cleaning your teeth, following the same underground route each day, or taking something exquisite, something which doesn't belong to you.

I pass one of our regulars on the red velour bench to my right with a *Melange*, a slice of *Sachertorte* and a copy of *Der Standard*.

'Gruss Gott,' I say.

He nods in return.

Greet God holds a familiar warmth for the Viennese. I pass the coat stand with its wooden swirls, hats dangling elegantly from the top hooks, and climb the stairs following the spiral up towards the next glass door which can swing either way. It confuses our customers.

Most take a window seat overlooking the street and the mural, except for the gentleman who comes in every Tuesday for a *Kleine Brauner* and a slice of *Pflaumen Streusel*. He sits in the corner seat, surrounded by deep pink, velour benches and flowered wallpaper from the late 1940s. He glances at the glass case wrapped around the kitchen. It draws in customers with elaborate tortes, all layered and topped with fruit, cream or swirls of chocolate. His face is a picture of lines and curves, his eyes twinkling as he orders the *Streusel*. I pass him a paper from the rack. He usually reads the local paper cover-to-cover in the time it takes him to drain his coffee cup and lick the last dusting of icing sugar from his lips, a wiping away of the final flurry of snow. He only speaks to the waitresses, rarely acknowledging other customers, and he tips generously. My tips are always larger than Katerin's.

'Liesl, you're early. Come and give me a hand.' Hans has been working here for barely a month but he appears to know everything about the place. He picks things up quickly, including girls.

'Yes,' I say with a smile, and I hang up my jacket in the back room, relieved not to have to peel off layers of clothing, along with gloves, hat and scarf. With my body blocking his view, I take out the scrap of paper and the star and slip them into the front pocket of my jeans. I pull my tunic down over the top.

'How was your weekend?' he asks, as I move back into the café.

'Good. I went to the Albertina. They've got a new exhibition.'

'You saw the Van Gogh exhibition?' he asks, his eyes widening.

Hans appears to share my love of art; a chameleon, moulding himself to suit the company he keeps. It makes most people feel comfortable around him, but it gives me a sense of unease. I don't know much about him, only that he's from Graz and has worked in London and the south of France, somewhere I can't recall. Maybe Nice, I forget. I suspect this is all I'll ever know. He's one of those people about whom you know everything and nothing: every piece of superficial detail, his need for an espresso before midday, his ability to retain historical facts and twelve-digit figures, his collection of mainly blue tops, and nothing about his family, his fears or hopes.

'Yes,' I say, 'that's the one. How did you know?'

He smiles. 'Because it's the only new exhibition on at the moment. What did you think of it?'

He asks too many questions for this time of day, but I answer, hoping it will curb his flow of enthusiasm.

'Good.'

'Just good? Any favourites?'

'Rain in Auvers. I find the lilacs pleasing. It makes sense to me.'

He nods and I wonder whether he understands. I take my apron from the peg and go to serve the two ladies who arrived after me and are now sitting by the window. I haven't seen them here before. I recognise a face anywhere if I've seen it once, and I can tell you the eye colour of anyone I've met. Hans has hazel-coloured eyes, mine are ice blue. My parents, apparently, had brown eyes. I inherited mine from my paternal grandfather, although I've never met him. I saw some old black-and-white photographs. I'd like to have been a photographer or a gallery curator. I slipped into the art world through the back door.

'What can I get you?' I ask.

'Do you have any fresh *Apfelstrudel*?'

'We do,' I say, pointing to the picture on the menu. 'It's here.'

'We'll take two slices and a *Melange*.'

I collect the menus as they fold away their glasses. They

must be tourists. Locals don't look at the menu, their personal tastes committed to memory. Although smaller than some of the more renowned cafés in the city, our history as the Royal Bavarian Court supplier to Emperor Franz Josef I draws in the more discerning tourists.

'Liesl, are you all right? You seem tense.' Hans' hand on my back makes me jump.

'Yes, I'm fine. Can you heat some strudel? I need two slices for the ladies by the window.'

'Yes,' he says.

I catch the beginnings of a frown as he turns away. I don't know why he is working here. He's smart and something doesn't quite fit, but he's charmed the rest of the staff. The café is beginning to fill its seats with elderly locals, a few tourists with museum pamphlets, children pressing their noses against the cake counter, and couples leaning in towards each other over steaming cups of coffee. The mirrored panelling on the side wall makes the place appear larger, duplicating customers in a kaleidoscopic spread of faces across the room: a Warhol painting of local life. I pull out my notebook and head towards customers who have waited longest, a family of four, all neatly dressed and could be Viennese. They look at me expectantly, like a nest of new starlings waiting to be fed.

'Do you know what you'd like?' I ask, then slip my hand into my pocket and clutch the star and the note. Still there. This is the fifth time I've checked since I left the cathedral. An image of the body invades my mind and I try to ignore it along with a growing sense of unease.

'Yes,' says the eldest of the baby starlings. She looks about ten years old. 'I'll have a hot chocolate and a croissant, please.' Her reason for choosing a croissant when there are plenty of colourful tortes on offer, is surprising. Maybe this is what she has for breakfast, a familiar routine.

'Of course,' I say, and I glance at the others with one eyebrow raised.

'Two cappuccinos for us and a slice each of the *Kardinal Schnitte*.' She speaks for her husband. The *Kardinal Schnitte* or Vatican Cake is a particular favourite for its light coffee-flavoured cream and meringue.

'Can I have an orange juice and the chocolate bomb thing?' I assume the youngest starling is referring to the *Sacherpunsch*, a Sachertorte soaked in rum and espresso. I look in the direction of the chocolate covered cakes to the right of the display, each piece emblazoned with our gold lettered topping, a king's seal. I'm not sure whether Daddy Starling knows that they're alcoholic but it's not my place to tell him.

'Is that all?' I ask, scanning the table.

They nod and I disappear into the kitchen to find Hans scooping the strudels onto blue-and-white china plates. He adds the cappuccinos and two glasses of cold tap water, loading them onto a silver tray with a panache I have yet to master, then carries them out balanced on one hand, leaving the door to swing shut.

I scan the kitchen, slip out into the ladies' room, lock the cubicle door behind me and stand up against the wall. I can feel my heartbeat – a slow, steady thud – and I imagine the blood, red and filled with oxygen as it courses through my body. I hear my breathing, heavy enough to make my fingertips tingle. My life is split into two parts, each ticks over to prevent me from becoming a corpse on the street to be walked over, belongings pilfered.

I dig into my pocket and pull out the star. It's identical

18

to those once owned by Empress Elisabeth but I don't yet know whether it's an original or a fake. I slide it back and pull out the note, relieved that it's typed. Most handwriting is almost illegible. Omama's words were often written in crude black ink with a plethora of swirls, dots and dashes, like a mediaeval manuscript. Her letters reminded me of the shape of the waves the moment before they break against the shore, before they pummel the sand into submission, eroding the form of the beach, grinding down shell and stone until they're barely recognisable.

Chapter 2

Liesl,

You will find Herr Schneider at Billrothstrasse 59. Knock firmly on the door or ring the bell three times. His hearing has been damaged and he may not hear you. Bring him a potted narcissi and bury the note deep into the soil. He will direct your next steps.

Albert

I know nothing of a Herr Schneider but I know the location of Billrothstrasse fifty-nine. I passed it on the number thirty-eight tram heading out towards Grinzing last week. My eyes were drawn to the large bay windows with vertical bars running from top to bottom. I noticed the house because it was set back off the road and it was more regal than the surrounding buildings which were modern and uncharacteristic of the city. I notice anything that stands out: a stray ear of corn blown down while the rest stand to worship the sun; a child in a bright outfit; a house with an air of aristocratic grandeur set amongst offices or derelict buildings. Some eyes spot the unfamiliar, objects out of place.

I've been away from the tables for all of four minutes, enough time to pile the order onto a silver tray and head back to the family of eager starlings waiting to be fed. When I reach the table they are folding the tablecloth at the corners, waiting. I'm sure I wasn't as patient as the youngest starling at the same age. I hand out drinks and cake, placing the chocolate bomb down with a smile. I scan the room, check the tables, and meet Hans coming out of the kitchen with another tray.

'Liesl, can you go downstairs? Ulrike need helps with the customers.'

'Of course,' I say.

I like to watch customers come and go, choosing cakes. I observe passers-by captivated by the window display – a fortress of tortes and sweet delights, topped with a seal of chocolate, engraved in gold with the signature name, Heiner, a statement of time, history and decadence. The display rotates through wedding cakes, Easter marzipan figures, Christmas gingerbread houses and fondant St Nikolauses. It's a box of delights for passing tourists and a familiar staple for regular customers.

'Thanks,' he says, 'I think you're better with the quick sales than the rest of us, and Ulrike likes you.'

'I'm not sure why. I don't have much to say until at least my second cup of coffee.' I head down the spiral staircase, keeping to the left as customers come up past me on the other side. The café stairs are stately looking, a reminder of a time when the minutes and hours were less hurried. I slide behind the counter downstairs, Ulrike catching my eye with a look of relief.

'Here, let me take this,' I say, and I finish wrapping three square boxes of Sachertorte for a burly American gentleman while Ulrike disappears into the back room.

'Thank you, Ma'am,' he says, his eyes twinkling with the

excitement of a child in a toy shop. 'I'll take a slice of each of these. What are they called?'

'*Esterházy Torte*, *Gugelhupf* and *Erdbeerschnitte*, Sir. If you don't mind me saying so, the Erdbeerschnitte is my favourite.'

'No problem,' he says with a jovial smile. 'They look good. I'll take two pieces and one of each of the others.'

He pats his stomach as customers behind begin to crowd forward. A woman in a hat glances at her watch. Others begin to shuffle. The ground floor is filling up, the queue pushing the front door wide open to extend out into the street. The crush of customers forming a line at the counter against a flow of people trying to exit is usual for a Saturday, but it's only Monday. Regulars sitting on the bench opposite are unfazed by the crowds, sipping espressos and lattes with their heads buried in papers.

I wrap the Heiner-inscribed cellophane around each slice, seal it with a crimson and gold sticker, lift each parcel onto the gold base with tongs and wrap the ends over into a basket handle. I never tire of seeing the look of anticipation on the face of a new customer. Looking up over the sea of heads, bags and hats, I spot Hans sauntering down the stairs. He glances across at me, smoothes his hand across the curve at the lower end of the stair rail and disappears into the back room. Both Hans and Ulrike resurface with boxes and more cake.

'Do you fancy a quick bite for lunch?' he asks.

'I suppose I can manage a short escape. Where do you want to go?'

'I know somewhere nearby. Come with me,' he says.

We gather our coats from the hooks upstairs. He holds mine out and I slip my arms into the sleeves, feeling his breath on my neck. His gesture doesn't surprise me, but his invitation is unexpected. He usually eats alone. He looks towards me briefly as we turn to leave. There is something about him that reminds me of someone on the run, a fugitive. He's not much taller than me, even when I'm wearing flats. I left my heels at home. I was running late and you can't run in them, not without twisting an ankle and ending up on the side of the pavement. I'd almost forgotten the body. He should have been alive when I reached him. I rarely find out what happened, pushing ahead with the plan, following instructions from Albert. I'm merely a puppet on a long string. I could never work alone, not with this type of work. We turn right before St Stephen's Cathedral.

'The restaurant's a few doors down on the right,' he says.

Hans's stride outstretches mine by at least half a step. He turns around before pushing open the door of a Japanese restaurant and leads me to a table around the corner. The staff nod towards him as we pass. He pulls out a chair for me and sits down opposite. His movements are swift and deliberate. I notice his nails, torn and bitten down, as though they were in the way. His eyes show caution in unexpected moments, his eyebrows neatly frame a square jaw and there is a hint of a dark shadow across his chin. He reminds me, absurdly, of a trained gun dog.

'What will you have?' he asks.

'Sushi. And you?'

'I'll go for the chicken and vegetable fried wok.'

A waiter approaches. They exchange a nod and he orders for both of us. I add a lemon soda and he asks for a cold beer. It's only twelve thirty and I don't want to let my guard down. A couple of beers loosen my tongue on an empty stomach. The problem with words is that you can't reel them back in. At school you could use the deft flick of a rubber and the sentence would be permanently removed. I tuck my bag under the table and pinch it between my ankles. Vienna is safe, but you never know. There are always one or two thrifty fingers waiting for a distracted customer. The food arrives swiftly.

'What do you do when you're not in the café?' he asks, tucking into the steaming stir-fry in front of him.

'All sorts of things. Art galleries, mainly.' I put the sushi back on the plate and fiddle with the chopsticks.

'So what did you think of the Albertina?'

I squint, trying to recall the weekend. 'It was good,' I say. I didn't go to the Albertina Museum, although I've been before and have committed the detail to memory. I'm careful to look up to my left for memory recall. Most people would never notice, but it's not worth leaving it to chance.

'I saw a black-and-white photography exhibition from the 1970s,' I hear myself say, the words leaving my lips in a flurry. This blatant fabrication of the truth is partly to convince myself of my supposed whereabouts.

'Have you seen the Van Gogh paintings at the museum in Amsterdam?'

'No, have you?' I should make the time to travel more often.

'Yes, it's one of my favourite galleries. His work is liberating to look at, don't you think?'

I imagine Hans walking along the canals of Amsterdam, past red light-infused windows with erotic dancers beckoning him in, and past tattoo parlours offering piercings of hearts and named lovers.

'I prefer Klimt,' I say. 'His work is in high demand at the moment.'

He nods with a wry smile. 'I could spend a day drifting through the rooms at the Belvedere. The gold, the shapes and the form of *Judith I* are mesmerising.'

I imagine his eyes lingering on the contours of her neck and lips. 'How much do you think it's worth?' I ask.

'*Landhaus am Attersee* sold for just over twenty-nine million dollars.'

A stray noodle escapes to the edge of his top lip and I resist the urge to say something. He wants me to know that he understands the art world. 'How do you know?' I ask.

He shrugs, 'I read. I remember figures. I probably saw it in the papers somewhere.' His tone is dismissive and I wonder which papers he reads - the international papers, *The New York Times*, *The Wall Street Journal* or maybe *Le Monde* or the *Financial Times*. I'd guess either *The Wall Street Journal* or the *Financial Times*. I imagine him in a pinstriped suit. Our burgundy work clothes give us anonymity, a collective identity stripped of individuality. When we walk through the glass doors each morning, we lose our other lives and become the property of Café Heiner. We smile, remain unfailingly polite and helpful, and are entirely professional. The customer is always right. Always.

'His work has fetched some of the highest prices in the business.' I say, hoping I might wrench him away from the caramelised vegetables drowning in soy sauce.

'Van Gogh?'

'Klimt.'

He puts his chopsticks down and leans in, resting on his left elbow. 'Well, that's an impressive fact.'

We both eat in silence. I circle the last few pieces of Maki. The delicate strips of prawn and avocado look too snug to be demolished. In a moment, the thin wall of seaweed encasing the rice and its contents will be severed between my teeth and vanish. The plate will transform into an empty space where there was once a swirl of patterns and shapes.

A waiter arrives, scoops up our plate and bowl and plants two ice cream menus down in front of us. The sheen of the plastic coating gives the ice cream an almost three-dimensional look and I wonder whether it's a sales tactic. The scent of lemongrass and coconut oil drifts from the kitchen and I watch the steam rise as it escapes through the gap between the metal counter and the overhead shelves.

The walls, I notice, are lime green. I should already know this. I've eaten here before, but today they strike me as being a shade too bright, too acidic. The tables around us begin to fill. A girl sits down opposite us with an older woman and they scan the ice cream menu. She looks no more than six years old and her red-and-white hair band matches her dress. Reams of fabric, I imagine, have gone into making the pleats and bows. I never wore anything pretty, only homogenous brown tops and trousers. Colourless. Lifeless. I like vibrancy and variety. She's fortunate to have a mother who dresses her in colour and brings her to places where she can try different foods.

Two men in suits are eating rice with chopsticks. Sushi is safer. You can delicately pick up a piece at a time without dropping rice or vegetables or staining the tablecloth with soy sauce. Hans picks up the top menu, his fingers hovering over the sundaes. I already know that I want the lemon sorbet so I leave the menu closed. He glances up at me, folds the menu and puts it down. His head tilts to one side and he waits expectantly.

'Sorbet. Lemon.' I say.

'Good. I'll have the full works,' he says. 'So where in

Austria are you from?' It's the first personal question he's asked.

'Vienna. I'm Viennese. Can't you hear the accent?'

'Yes. Yes, of course, a true *Wienerin*.'

'And you?'

'Graz,' he says, almost as though it's a question.

'Yes,' I say, 'I think you told me once before.'

I hear two chefs arguing behind the shelving and watch one bend down and pick up a pan with his fist clamped around the handle, waving the other hand through the steam. I can't see the other chef.

'Don't worry. It's not the most exciting thing about me.'

'What did you study?' I ask, ignoring his prompt.

'Politics and Economics.'

'That must've kept you busy,' I say.

'It's useful and I enjoyed it. What about you?'

'Art History, here in Vienna.' This sounds considerably less academic.

'So you're an art lover and not just on the weekends.'

'My grandfather was a painter and my grandmother was an art historian. I spent much of my time with them as a child. I remember the smell of the oil paints and damp turpentine-infused cloths. She had books with photographs of old buildings and paintings of the masters.'

He is looking directly at me, listening intently. His eyes never break their gaze to look over my shoulder or to check his watch.

Chapter 3

A storm cloud threatens to open the skies above the ring. I decide to walk the route of the No 1 tram, circling the city centre. I prefer to walk, it refreshes my senses. The most striking buildings are along this route and I can see them better on foot. I turn right out of Heldenplatz and walk the perimeter. You can take a shortcut through the park with its scent of roses, but I like the museum view where trams clickety-clack as they pass over joints in the tracks. The traffic has picked up and the beginnings of a tourist flurry are evident. Oriental travellers with video cameras and zoom lenses and American and Canadian accents can be heard in the crowds. It's not always easy for an Austrian to tell the two apart. They photograph the gateway into the Hofburg Palace – a regal display of arches and grandeur.

The Natural History Museum to my left mirrors the History of Art Museum that sits exactly opposite. The History of Art Museum was the scene of an art theft, the largest heist in Austria: the *Saliera*, a gold Cellini salt cellar, the *Mona Lisa* of sculptures. It was taken from the museum's Hapsburg collection by a man in the early hours of the morning. His entry point seems even more improbable than the Dulwich Picture Gallery case in London. He climbed up the scaffolding and broke in through a window. They say the security guard missed it but I imagine he was in on the deal. Security guards don't miss these events, they don't forget to switch on the lights for the cameras to pick up activity or avoid investigating a noise. It's simply careless.

I digress. The law courts are the next building along the ring, set slightly further back from the road. They know how to use security systems. The entrance has airport-style security with two fully encased cylinders designed to close in on every entrant. They scan every inch of the body, picking up outlines of sharp or explosive objects. It creates a momentary feeling of entrapment before the curved glass doors open up, propelling the visitor into an entrance with a high glass ceiling, a stone staircase and layers of arches and ornate design. I take security systems as seriously as I do art. I should have been a computer analyst or something useful.

The parliament building, a Romanesque building with columns and gold-leaf frescos, is further along the ring. A fountain separates sweeping entrances on both sides of the road. Security is tight. I curve to the right, passing the Rathaus, a town hall with gothic spires protruding through trees. The Burgtheater is on the opposite side, with sumptuous gardens and rows of people sitting on benches as they watch their children run through the rose beds. I spend my afternoons in lectures at the university, the building beyond the Rathaus. My job at Café Heiner, along with a security job in the evenings and at weekends at the Leopold Museum, allow me to study.

As I reach Schottentor station and wait for the tram, I see a homeless man trying to feed his dog. The sweet stench of the kebab stand makes me retch. I take a few steps towards the tracks. The No 38 tram rolls down into Schottentor before curving back on itself. I wait for passengers to climb down the steps before getting on and finding a seat by the back window. I face the rear of the train and am in the last carriage. I have a clear view. I put my feet up on the ledge in front, slip my headphones on, clasp the star brooch, and close my eyes.

I must remember to pick up a narcissus plant and push the note down into the soil. Herr Schneider must know Albert, or at least know of him. I imagine Albert as a clandestine figure who is never seen, smokes a pipe and gives orders via a carefully organised network as he directs large, illicit operations. Or he's an older man with a steely gaze perhaps, with half-glasses and a tweed jacket, masquerading as a legitimate businessman. The thought of the former makes me shudder and I change tracks, listening instead to Miles Davis. My nerves rarely catch me off guard but the thought of meeting Herr Schneider, and intrusive images of the body at the top of the steps of the underground station, have made me jittery.

I pull a discarded chewing gum wrapper from my pocket, stretch it out and twist it into a totem pole of letters in green and white. I spin it between the index and second finger of my right hand. It releases some tension. I feel afraid for the first time in months although I'm not sure why. A momentary inability to remember the number of Herr Schneider's house betrays me. I should remember. I never forget a detail: a name, a number, a place. I can't remember whether the stop is Gatterburggasse or Silbergasse. Gatterburggasse is too early. I need the next stop. The tram stops again and empties at Hardtgasse which means there are two more stops. We pass a bar, a video shop, a few takeaway restaurants, the university halls of residence and the *Apotheke*. I still don't know what I will say to Herr Schneider and I don't know why Albert has sent me. I tell myself that my life won't be at risk. I don't know why the man at the station wasn't alive when I reached him and I wonder, for a moment, whether Herr Schneider will be alive when I reach number fifty-nine. I remember now, it's fifty-nine.

The tram judders as it stops. The brakes screech as the steel wheels resist the pressure. I stay on the tram for one stop beyond number fifty-nine the potted narcissus. There's a flower stall in front of the Rudolfinerhaus hospital where I was born. The tram waits at the lights. I turn to watch them until the red is replaced by flashing amber – a warning – then by green. The carriages begin their descent from Billrothstrasse and around the corner, stopping at Silbergasse. I look both ways and cross the tracks towards the flower stall. I enter but can't see any narcissi. The assistant looks at the back of the shop and pulls one out from behind a flower arrangement.

I pay and wonder whether to get on the tram travelling in the opposite direction back to the previous stop but decide instead to walk. The day is fresh and I draw the air deep into my lungs. Holding the plant in my left hand, I rearrange my shoulder bag with the other hand. It slips, irritatingly, when I walk. This only happens when I wear a jacket. It stays in place when I am only wearing a light top. I realise I am not out of breath, despite the ascent, and put that down to the increased distance in my runs. I've pushed myself from ten kilometres to fifteen and my fitness is building. It's important to keep my body lean and to be able to move fast.

I stop outside number fifty-nine without looking at the numbers. I recognise the bars and the bay windows. The house isn't particularly noticeable and, set back off the road, reminds me of a remote Scottish Highlands castle. I've often wondered about the owner.

I see the curtain move. He is expecting me. There's no need to ring the bell three times. I reach the front door and press once. Nothing happens. I ring again. Silence. I ring for a third time and hear footsteps walking along what sounds like a wooden corridor. I hold up the pot with its yellow bloom, pull the note from my pocket and plunge it deep into the soil as the handle turns. The face of a man about my height peers through the chink in the door.

'Herr Schneider,' I say. 'Liesl Baumgartner.'

'Liesl who?'

'Baumgartner.' I suspect he heard me the first time.

'Come in.' He motions with his hand for me to enter quickly, as though I might have been followed.

He opens the door and I place one foot inside the house followed by the other. The hall smells musty and airless and I wonder if he lives alone. At first glance, it looks as though he might, but you can't always tell. Some people surprise me. Some houses surprise me. He takes the narcissus and pokes his fingers down into the soil, then pulls out Albert's note and shakes it. Several soil particles loosen from the paper and fly through the air. He picks up a stick from a tall coat rack with curled wooden arms formed in a willow-tree shape, its branches drawing down towards the floor. He slides the note into his pocket, turns on his heels and disappears down the corridor. I wonder whether to follow and decide it would be better than standing in the hallway.

There is a tall grandfather clock further along to the left, a collection of antique maps on the other side, and a row of Klimt sketches. These are originals and I wonder why they are on display in such a visible location. He must be aware of their value. The walls are covered with frames. Some contain black-and-white portraits, possibly of family members, others encase detailed watercolours and small tapestries. The walls are high, vanishing into a white ceiling a few metres above my head. He mutters words I can't hear and continues to walk. I follow until he reaches the kitchen.

'Coffee,' he announces, more as a statement than a question. He turns to look at me and I shudder, as though I've stepped across a grave and awakened a spirit. I nod enough to form a yes, knowing he'll make one anyway, two if he joins me. His stature is upright for a man of his age and his eyes are steely and searching. His eyebrows are wispy with flashes of white and the lines of his face draw downwards, sloping towards an angular chin. His face has been chiselled with the knife of a fine carpenter and his nose stops short of being hooked. He wears a frown, which appears accidental, a sign of time and pressure. There's a resoluteness to his voice, making his opinions sound like facts. He forms no open questions at this stage and I'm relieved, but I know his mind is searching for answers beyond my note and Albert's. Elderly people make me uncomfortable, especially elderly people who don't speak. I presume he knows Albert and this alone makes me tense. Each minute in his house edges closer to the time when I can leave.

'Have you always lived here?' I ask, wondering whether the question will be shrugged off, along with all the other unnecessary irritations of life.

'All my life. I was born in that room.' He points diagonally upwards to what must be one of the bedrooms. There are five doors leading from the hallway which suggests that there are five substantial rooms above us.

'And your siblings? Do you have brothers or sisters?'

'A sister. My brother died.'

'I'm sorry,' I say. These are the only words I can summon.

'It's ok. He was found at Stephansplatz station at the top of the steps.' He stares into my eyes and tries to hold my gaze. 'He was due to meet somebody. We don't know who. The items he had on him were missing.'

The image of the body paralyses me, leaving me unable to speak. The word *we* lingers in my mind. It feels as though a hand is gripping my throat. Does he know I should have met him? Does he know about the brooch and the note? I no longer feel safe and I wonder if he has his suspicions, or whether Albert has already incriminated me. I didn't feel entirely safe when I arrived, even less so now. His eyes are still fixed on mine and the note sits in his pocket, taken from the trousers of his own flesh and blood. I cut the stream of thoughts before they reach a conclusion.

'It must have been a shock.' I manage to force the words out of my mouth, my lips so dry they smack together when I speak. 'For you, I mean. Are these yours?' I point to some paintings by my chair. They have a signature on the lower right that I don't recognise. The style differs from all the other paintings in the house.

His face lights up. 'Yes, I used to paint. Now I collect other people's paintings.' He nods enough for me to notice and I acknowledge his comment.

'You have quite a collection. Are those Klimts?' I ask, pointing in the direction of the hall.

He nods again, without any explanation. 'Kuchen?' he asks.

I imagine fine cakes and pastries but my stomach is rolling and I feel too tense to eat.

'No, coffee is fine.' I don't want to drag out my stay any longer than necessary.

'I expect you want to know about the note.' His tone is free of emotion.

'If it's necessary.' I acquire information on a need-to-know basis.

'Very well. I'll assume you don't need to know this time.'

I immediately regret my last comment but refuse to show further interest. I drain the coffee cup and get up to leave.

'Thank you. I'll head back into town.'

'Was there anything with the note?'

'No,' I say, hoping my words prove convincing. Albert's note said nothing about handing over the diamond brooch, only the note itself. The brooch is tucked away in the apartment. He nods, stands up, and plants a note in my coat pocket. His eyes close in on me, searching mine for any information he can draw. I turn, make my way to the door and feel him follow me out of the room. His footsteps are close behind and his pace only marginally slower.

'Before you go, can you tell me what he was wearing when you saw him?' I freeze. 'It's all right,' he says, 'you don't need to be afraid. I know Albert sent you.'

This doesn't put me at ease. He speaks about his brother with a disconnect, as though the string of events – the body, the note, my meeting here – are a passing thought. I should be used to this kind of approach but I find his apparent indifference chilling.

'I don't remember. I took the note and made my way out of the station. I'm sorry for your loss. He should have been alive.' He is silent. His face reveals nothing I recognise as grief. He looks through me, out towards the window into the street beyond. A tram rumbles past.

'I'll get going. Thank you.' I say, swallowing most of the sentence. Only the word *going* sounds intelligible.

My hands and feet are tingling, fizzing almost. I try not to break into a sprint as he releases me from the house. It feels cold, despite the warmth of the day. I raise a hand to say goodbye, not wanting to turn back or look into his eyes. I can feel them piercing me and I focus on the gate and the black iron rails curling and twisting like a dark thicket of weed.

Tram 38 arrives. I get on and the door closes behind me. I walk through the gate as if shaking off a swarm of flies. I turn right and walk down to the stop by Chimanistrasse, but the tram takes off at the lights at high speed without waiting for anyone. If it had waited a while longer I could have made my escape. Waiting outside the Hochriegel champagne factory, the scent of fermentation is tantalising.

The next tram reaches the brow of the hill seven minutes later, slowing as it reaches the stop. It should have only been five. A few people are pacing and looking at their watches. Any delay longer than a minute is late. I'm flanked on one side by an elderly lady with a wicker shopping trolley on wheels and on the other by a boy in baggy trousers with oversized headphones. He can't hear the tram but we can all feel the vibrations beneath our feet. He looks up before it draws to a halt. I climb the steps as the doors open and help the lady with the trolley.

The doors close automatically as I head towards the back of the tram and find a seat facing the rear. I put my feet up on the ledge and put my own earbuds into my ears. They are small and inconspicuous. Sometimes I remove one so that I can hear everything: my music and the outside world. My eyes are drawn upwards towards the skylights of the buildings looming over the street. The clouds have darkened. I close my eyes, the beat bringing the rhythm of my pulse to a steadier pace. The sound of the wheels on the tracks vanishes.

I pull out the note from Herr Schneider, lines of black ink typed and printed to avoid any flow of character from reaching the page.

Go to the bible collection in the library on Tuesday morning at 10am. Deposit the Van Gogh inside a King James and leave.

Chapter 4

The following morning, I take a tram to the National Library, get off at Albertinaplatz and walk briskly along Josefsplatz until I reach the courtyard with the statue of a lion. He looks at me with disdain. The doors to the main entrance tower over me with giants and the imperial double-headed eagle guarding the entrance. I suspect they'll turn a blind eye to my arrival. Part of the Hofburg Palace, this houses one of the largest collections of Martin Luther's writings and is arguably one of the most beautiful libraries in the world, but is mostly visited by tourists. The job should be quick. It's relatively quiet. I slip in and walk slowly to the main library room, trying not to draw any attention. I've already checked the building for entrances, exits, guards, cameras – the usual. I need to know everything: timings, opening and peak hours, number of personnel on the ground, shift cycles. Observe everything, pre-plan, check everything, know your route in and out. I'm right on time, as always. Today, luck is on my side. I can feel it in the pit of my stomach, the thrill of the risk, coupled with the knowledge that I can pull this off. Van Gogh's *Beach at Scheveningen in Stormy Weather*, tucked inside the book in the base of my bag, my jacked draped over the opening. Unlike galleries, there's no need to hand anything in. I walk towards the next set of doors, passing a couple of Japanese tourists, both with single-lens reflex cameras around their necks and an array of lenses slotted into padded camera bags, the real deal. He's wearing walking trousers and a tee shirt, she looks elegant in tailored linen trousers, a pressed shirt and floral scarf. A travel-sized city map pokes out of a small rucksack on his back and I wonder whether they'll find the city's backstreets with their antique dealers tucked inside ancient buildings, shielded from the heat of the sun. Seasoned buyers and exclusive gallery dealers know their location but travellers rarely find them or make an effort to blend in, continually harassed by ticket sellers outside the Opera House and the Cathedral. They stand out more in winter than in summer. Locals wrap up in coats as thick as sleeping bags with fur-lined hoods and thick hats and gloves, while tourists are mostly British or American and wear thin autumn jackets and flimsy umbrellas. They expect rain and are prepared for all weather except for the extreme cold of Austrian winters. Our summers turn to winters and back again with little in between. Spring and autumn are gone in a flash, if they arrive at all.

I pass a guard. He fails to notice me or my bag with the jacket slung across it. I let out a long, slow breath. You get used to the manoeuvres, but the surge of adrenalin never leaves you – the scent of excitement, a whiff of danger. I know that what I'm undertaking is wrong but it's all I know. And besides, I no longer care for the rules. There are days when waitressing is harder, more gruelling. I hate the mundane. I live for the quick thrills and danger, the risk of getting caught. I need to know I can achieve the unachievable, rattle a few cages, including my own. It's thrilling to hold a ten million euro painting in your bag like a heap of groceries, to carry art into a library and locate a dead drop. I must follow Albert's instructions. We've never actually met but I follow his every wish to the last detail: the library, the King James.

I found a King James Bible large enough in a second-hand bookshop. I cut out the pages last night and reinforced the edges of the spine. I don't think God will mind and I doubt Albert cares. I created a false edging to replace the page leaves and inserted the rolled up Van Gogh. I had a good look at the painting first. It's beautiful but I can't keep it. I discovered it was housed in the Van Gogh Museum in Amsterdam before eventually being passed on to me. I don't know how many times it has changed hands since its removal from the museum. I picked it up from a dead drop in the Hofburg last week. It hadn't been easy, too many tourists and guards, and had been tucked behind a painting of Empress Sissi in one of the rooms. The fine details of the white hats on the women by the shore, the small red flag of the sailing boat billowing in the wind, storm clouds rolling in, the frenetic movement of the waves and the way the low light catches them as they break, bring the whole scene to life. You can almost feel the movement of the water. I unravelled it and watched it as I drank a shot of vodka and smoked my last Memphis. I had to find a large enough version of the King James to roll it up into – thirty-four point five centimetres, to be exact. The width of the painting has to fit the length of the bible. The location of the dead drop in the library matters. At least Albert didn't pick the oldest bible in the library to switch with – the 1368 golden Holy Gospels. That would be sacrilege.

Stepping into the ceremonial room takes your breath away. I'm watched by the cupola ceiling frescos. Quiet glances from the cherubs cast a shadow of doom across my path momentarily. I observe the statue of Karl VI, the Holy Roman

Emperor. He appears to be welcoming. I'd like to have met his daughter and Hapsburg ruler, Maria Theresa. She had the same strength and steely determination as I do. She got things done. I remind myself he knows nothing of my intentions to remove any items and I head towards the back end of the room. The scent of old books fills my lungs as I breathe deeply, inhaling history. Some of the manuscripts are from the fourth century BC. I feel a shiver of excitement being inside a part of the Hofburg Palace with over seven million items of value within my reach, and the fact that I'm concealing a priceless Van Gogh makes me shudder. I wish I'd been the one to lift it from Amsterdam. I sometimes try to imagine what's happened, the route a painting has taken and how it has reached me, where it goes from here. I never know whether or not it will change hands a few more times before it reaches its final destination. It's harder to sell stolen works and they only garner a fraction of their open market value but it remains a lucrative business. I'm in it for the thrill as much as the money. Most galleries aren't well guarded, and it helps if you know the timings the way that I do in the Leopold. It's easy to figure out in any gallery if you look for long enough. Observation is important, observation of people, their movements, patterns, irregularities. It builds a picture that helps a criminal to slip into the shadows.

The dead drop last month, to collect a Dutch landscape, took me to the Papyrus Collection in the Neue Burg wing of the Hofburg Palace with its clay and stone tablets and bronze-inscribed objects: windows to a sumptuous and mysterious past. The hieroglyphs symbolise the artistry and accuracy of an ancient civilisation, a people of Gods, shrouded in the beliefs of the afterlife. Omama taught me about Abu Simbel during the cold winter nights. She spoke of the tombs and the sun as it shone through the temple of Rameses II onto the God Osiris. She said it proved humans were capable of anything. I plan to visit the tombs one day when I'm free from this way of life. The landscape, *Landscape with Obelisk* by Dutch Golden Age artist, Govert Finck, was hidden in a wooden wall panel of one of the quieter rooms, away from cameras. The irony of the title and the location was not lost on me. It was apparently taken from the Boston collection. I could collect the reward money, but it would take me out of the game. Passing it on will be the next job after this.

Here, in the ceremonial room, a breathtaking eighty metres long and twenty metres high, and built in the eighteenth century as part of the former Court Library, I have sixteenth century maps, three hundred and eighty globes, two hundred thousand books and Strauss' scores at my fingertips. All priceless. There are four incredible Venetian globes, each with a diameter of over a metre. This place is perfect. I keep my head down and I walk towards the back of the room, passing row upon row of ancient manuscripts, all beautifully bound in leather. The room itself is a baroque masterpiece with its sumptuous walls, adorned with art and ladders reaching up to the heavens. I look skyward, the sunlight illuminating the figures stretching from eight high windows towards the centre of the ceiling, rivalling the Sistine Chapel. The image of Charles VI held up by Hercules and Apollo displays an array of colours. The figure of eternal glory at the centre holds an honour symbol, a triangle, in his right arm. The outer circle displays vices and marks a transition to the secular world, a world where criminals steal paintings and post them in dead drops right under their noses, before returning to café life. I have a magpie-like compulsion to collect treasures, the rarer and the more difficult to lift, the better. This is why I was hired. People don't usually suspect a young woman, and I can charm any guard who might start to ask too many questions. It's only happened once, just before the Rembrandts were taken from the Dulwich Picture Gallery in London. I wasn't involved, but I was impressed by the operation. There are rumours surrounding the perpetrators but not the method or the capture. They removed the wood panels to enter and exit. Not very subtle in my view, but it worked.

I scan the room, pull out the King James and replace it with my own chiselled out version containing the Van Gogh. I stifle the urge to sneeze as dust particles explode into the air. The whole operation is done in two swift movements, one book out and one replacement put back in the gap. I slide the original under my coat and into the bag, and wander over to the globe to take a closer look. This particular bible will be sold for a considerable price and it won't make its way back to the library. I know not to rush out. It's important that my activity doesn't stand out from the people around me, whether in a gallery, a library, a café or on the underground. I need to look plain and inconspicuous.

My shift at the Leopold Gallery is quiet this evening. The shuffle of feet normally winds down to a steady trickle by five which is when I begin most of my shifts. Today, I'm on the lower level in the vaults of the gallery. The descent in the lift to the second floor below ground reminds me of the underground tunnels. The doors open up to a bright entrance hall with a high ceiling. The exhibitions on this level vary which makes our jobs more interesting. The temporary exhibitions hold an element of surprise against the familiarity

43

of the permanent collections. The Klimts are unique, but when I see a new collection for the first time, I feel expectation, a hope of enchantment, or simply the need to be left breathless.

I watch the few who remain as the lift leaves the floor. Circling the entrance hall, visitors read abstracts on the walls, linger by a certain picture, scan leaflets picked up on the way into the gallery. An elderly man leans in towards a Warhol print and I wonder if this really is his style. He hovers over the image. I begin to move towards him to ask him to step away, but he takes two or three steps backwards and squints, lifting his glasses an inch. He sits down on the long bench in the middle of the room, rests his elbows on his knees and lowers his head into his hands. He reminds me of a schoolboy investigating a science exhibit. He looks to his left, as if to speak, and I wonder if he is used to sharing the experience with someone who's no longer in his life. There's a sadness in his eyes, a hint of loss, a shadow of something or someone. His movements are gentle and it strikes me then that he may have fought during the war. I wonder how his life might have changed over the decades, and how mine will change before I reach his age. I snap out of this train of thought and walk towards the next room. It's time to rotate rooms. I can't imagine ever being in a relationship.

'Can you tell me where the Egon Scheile paintings are?' asks a girl, who looks a little younger than me. She stuffs the flyer for the Warhol exhibition into a satchel and looks at me expectantly.

'Up on the second floor,' I say, tilting my head upwards.

'Thank you. And the gift shop?'

'First floor,' I say.

She nods and disappears towards the lift. An elderly couple is sitting on the bench, but they look out of place. People's taste in art can be as unexpected as finding a butterfly in a beehive, or watching the onset of a storm over calm waters. A dealer in France may order an ancient Inca artefact and a collector in Italy might request a specific Finnish painting. I once collected a Japanese sketch for a Scandinavian operation. Time has taught me that in life, you can predict very little about the tastes and behaviours of others. Some aspects of life are more predictable: the ebb and flow of visitors to a gallery or the National Library, the opening of the cathedral each day, the burning of incense before prayer, absolution.

I hear a shout and turn to see an elderly lady on the bench get down on the floor to where her husband is lying. Her bag sits alone on the bench. Only a thief notices these things. I rush over as other visitors crowd in, wanting to see what has happened. I radio for help, ask people to stand back, then check his airway and feel for a pulse. I can feel the gentle pounding of his blood supply, but he isn't conscious. His body rolls grudgingly into the recovery position as I lift and pull his knee.

'Please stay calm,' I say to a young woman who is becoming hysterical and I look at the man's elderly wife to reassure her. 'He'll be ok. Hold his hand and talk to him.' I've learned to rely on no one, but we all need someone in that moment when life fades, spins out of control – a quiet voice, a hand on a shoulder, a reassuring word. I stand up and tell people to step back. I need to disperse the crowd that has formed. Several guards exit the lift. They head in our direction and I explain the sequence of events leading up to finding his body lying lifeless on the floor. His wife looks anxious. I lift her bag and place it beside her. It feels light, almost weightless. The guards nod and it's only another ten minutes before two paramedics arrive in luminous suits with a stretcher. The gallery has been cleared when his body is lifted onto it. As they carry him towards the lift, my thoughts turn towards the body at Stephansplatz.

I get back to my apartment late this evening. Nothing has been disturbed. I pull out the King James that I retrieved from the National Library to find another note from Albert.

Liesl,

Take the Obelisk painting to St. Peter's next Tuesday at 8am, before Mass. Slide it under the bench on the right, third row back and leave. Pray if you must.

Albert

Chapter 5

I leave the cathedral this morning with the Obelisk painting hidden deep inside my bag. The thought that I am carrying a priceless work of art gives me an incomparable thrill and the fact that nobody knows makes it even more exhilarating. I turn the corner on to Graben but can feel someone close on my tail. I know when I'm being followed. It's always a hunch and I'm rarely wrong.

Turning to look into a shop window, I glimpse two police uniforms out of the corner of my eye. I wait a few more seconds, then walk further along Graben until I reach the turning for St. Peter's church on my right. The footsteps are closing in so I step inside, hoping it'll be safer here in the crowd gathered for morning mass. The music gives me peace even if it doesn't come from my own lips. I sit down on a bench towards the front to pray, hoping the officers haven't followed me inside. They're here, but they haven't seen me. I take off my coat and pull a hat from my bag, forcing the grey felt down over my curls, teasing each side down below the tips of my ears. You learn to find ways of disguising yourself. I can't turn around and it's not safe to deposit the painting, not yet. I bow my head, say a prayer and leave.

I take the route behind the church along Milchgasse, but they follow. I turn a corner to my right, remove the painting from my bag and plunge it deep into a rubbish bin. It's easier to deposit the work when it's rolled up. You can slide it behind books or ease it into narrow spaces. Some clients don't care if it's damaged at the edges, but I care.

Breathless, and with my heart racing, I enter the café, sit with my back against the wall, feet stretched out in front of me. Taking deep breaths, I place a half empty bag down on the coffee table. It still holds my scarf, a cardigan and other bits of disguise, in case I need them.

The waiter walks over with his notepad and pen, without looking up.

'I'll have an espresso,' I say.

He nods and disappears behind the counter. There is an array of cakes but none are as enticing as ours. The place is quiet and I pick up a paper, shaking it out and holding it so that it almost covers my face. Two officers walk past the window. This is the first time I've been followed and it won't be the last. I look up again as the waiter arrives with the coffee, and I see Hans. Unnervingly, he turns into the café and comes over to my table.

'Oh, hello,' he says, pulling out a chair. 'Mind if I join you?'

'Of course.' I put the paper down, folding it neatly, and take a sip of hot coffee, cupping the glass to steel my nerves.

He signals to the waiter and orders an espresso, then looks at me. 'You know you only have to ask. I could have made you a coffee myself.'

I smile and wonder if he has followed me. 'I've finished my shift and I like the espressos here, they're stronger.' There's an edge to him that doesn't let me rest. Aware that the painting is still in the bin, I jump up. 'I need to get some cigarettes. I'll be back in a minute,' I say.

'I've got one. Here,' he says, offering me a Marlboro.

'It's all right. I need to pick up a prescription before the Apotheke closes for lunch.'

'Sure. I'll come with you.'

'No,' I say, abruptly, then I lower my tone. 'I can go alone.'

He gives me a look that I can't discern, then picks up the paper and leans back into his chair. I pull an old prescription out of my bag. Outside on the pavement, I let the air fill my lungs. It's been a morning of close encounters: the security guard who watched me for longer than usual, the tourists who blocked my path to the painting, the officers along Graben, and now Hans. His path has crossed with mine on several occasions in recent weeks. I think I saw him leave the library as I swapped the King James bibles but he looks like many other twenty-five year old European boys. There's nothing unusual about his looks that would make him stand out in a lineup, although he looks too clean-cut for the art underworld.

I head back towards the bin, making sure that I've lost the police officers, scan the route both ways, put an empty pack of cigarettes in the bin and pull out the painting. I slide it carefully into my bag, then drape my coat over the top. The church is filling up. I slip in through the main doors and move towards the third row on the right. I kneel down to pray, grateful not to see any of the same faces. Twice in one morning might make it look as though I need some assistance. I lean over the bag, pull out the painting and hide it under the bench. I look up to see who is about and run my hand along the underside of the bench, stopping as I reach an envelope attached with a small piece of tape. I pull it off and tuck it away in my pocket, then leave to go home and change for another cafe shift.

I'm grateful to get back to the apartment. A bowl with

an apple core and orange peel is still on the kitchen counter from this morning. The pot beneath the percolator is filled with cold coffee. I decide against reheating it and tip it down the sink, then head into the living room to find a spot on the sofa. I pull the note from my bag and unseal it. The envelope is not one I've seen before. It's a different envelope to Albert's and Herr Schneider's, longer and thinner, like an AirMail envelope, but white.

Liesl,

Go to Schönbrunner Schlosstrasse tomorrow morning at 10:30am, and knock on the door of the apartment to the left of the main entrance to the Palace. Get to know Maria and learn from her.

It is unsigned and may, or may not, be from Albert. I need to keep track of the notes, locations and the information given, so that I can stay a step ahead and not slip up. 'Learn from her,' sounds ominous. I have no idea who wrote the note or why they want me to meet a lady called Maria, but I need to follow orders. I change into my uniform, pull up the window and light a cigarette. The city is gradually filling up with visitors and residents returning from mountain retreats. I feel the first signs of autumn in the air as I watch the leaves of the beech tree, burnished at the edges, twist and curl, readying themselves to shed for winter. The magnolia across the road is turning golden. I don't miss the pinks when the colours are this beautiful. The shedding of leaves reminds me of the constancy of letting things go and of the beauty in leaving behind the old.

I stub out the cigarette, half-smoked, and leave the

apartment, locking the door behind me. The shift at the cafe is a whirl of customers, mostly asking about the markets. I've been asked to arrange the gingerbread houses and marzipan fruits in the windows to create an enticing display. People on Kärntner Strasse stop to watch the scene unfolding from outside, children press their faces against the glass, point to the scene I'm creating and shout with excitement. The anticipation is palpable at this time of year. Few can avoid it. I don't see Hans in the cafe, or Katerin or Ulrike.

Is Hans still following up on my movements near Graben?

Chapter 6

I head out the next morning to the cafe at the end of my street and grab an espresso and a croissant. It's rare that I eat anything in the mornings but I don't remember eating last night. This place is more of a bakery with a couple of tables and chairs out on the street, than an actual cafe, but it's quiet. I sit outside and breathe in the scent of autumn. I don't get enough daylight, spending more time in darkness than in the light. I take a cigarette from a new pack, light it, and lean back into the metal seat, watching trams as they pass. The streets are a lattice of overhead wires, connecting trams to power, with two hundred and ninety-two kilometres of tracks spread out across the city. On a map, it looks like a Japanese spider crab crawling towards the Danube. They are considered a delicacy in Japan, and are at risk of overfishing. Anything that is considered unique becomes valuable, and is either collected or snatched. I down the espresso shot, stub out the cigarette in the ashtray on the table and wipe pastry flakes from my top. A couple with a double buggy pass me as I get up. I wait before crossing the road to get the tram to the underground at Schönbrunn. I wonder whether Albert might have sent me to her, or Herr Schneider or, perhaps, someone else entirely.

The train clunks to a halt at Schönbrunn, close to the palace gates. I leave the carriage and climb the stairs up to street level. The sun's rays catch the edges of each step leading up into the light and out onto the street. People swirl about, mostly heading towards the palace entrance. Large coaches pull up in bays on the side of the road. It can be busier here than in the city centre. Tourists arrive to see the palace all year round, with its deep yellow walls and sweeping Rococo staircases, but it's especially busy in August and September. A little known fact, the name Schönbrunn comes from an artesian well that was used by the court.

Tulip-filled gardens, the maze and the oldest zoo in the world, all housed in the palace complex, pull in crowds. Established by the Hapsburgs in 1752, the zoo was set up by Empress Maria Theresa's husband, Franz I, who would visit the zoo after morning Mass. A progressive thinker of his time, his interest in science and nature and his natural history collections provided the foundation for Vienna's Natural History Museum.

The best cakes in the city can be found in the Gloriette, the glass house at the end of the palace gardens. I picture Empress Elisabeth riding on horseback for a sumptuous afternoon tea and sweeping views of the place and the city beyond with the Stephansdom Cathedral spire. There were no art deals or stolen greats in her time, not the way there are now with their high auction prices and high demand in the Art underworld.

Maria's apartment stands a couple of metres from the street, across a small lawn. All of the buildings match the yellow of the palace. Rows of doors and windows stretch out towards the main gates. It's ten thirty, exactly. I cross over to the other side of the road, knock tentatively on the first door and stand back. A woman answers.

'Maria?' I ask.

'Yes, dear. You must be Liesl. Come in.' She is clearly expecting me. 'You're right on time.'

'Thank you,' I say, following her through a narrow hallway and left into a cosy sitting room filled with pictures and shelves of photographs and ornaments. She looks well-travelled. Her gaze gives me a sense of unease as she looks me up and down.

'Coffee?' she asks.

'Yes, thank you.' I don't ask her who sent me. I suspect she won't say. She leaves the room and returns with a tray.

'Have a seat,' she says.

I hesitate then sit down opposite her. 'Thank you.'

She pours the coffee, passes me a cup and pulls a piece of paper from her pocket, unfolding it gently. She passes me a beautiful old hand-drawn, three-dimensional map of the city. I recognise the Volksgarten, the Sigmund Freud Park by the Town Hall, the Burgtheater, and the Concert House, my favourite building, a grand presentation for some of the best symphony performances. The buildings stand out from the smaller shops, offices, spires and domes, nestled under the southern banks of the Danube canal. All the roads radiate out from the cathedral at the centre, its spire overshadowing all other buildings in the central radius, although I can also see the dome of St. Peter's. My eyes are drawn to the star encompassing the church. I notice more stars, all hand drawn and scattered across the map like the first flutter of snowflakes landing across a path.

'Do you like it?' she asks, looking at me earnestly.

'It's beautiful. What do the stars represent?' I hand her the map and point to the star by the Musikverein. She grins and, for a moment, she looks like a schoolgirl, her face lit up in anticipation. I wait.

'I was hoping you'd ask,' she says, her eyes glinting. 'These were the places where we went together.'

'We?' I ask, knowing she'll tell me more.

'Yes. His name was Karl.' She lowers her head. 'He was a Nazi soldier. My parents wouldn't allow it. I met him during the Anschluss. Look.' She points to the star around Sigmund Freud Park. 'He took me to the Christkindlemarkt. It was beautiful. I can still remember the calendar windows in the arches of the Rathaus, all lit up and full of promise ... a promise of Christmas, of the future. I was naïve. The lights and the smell of roasted nuts and pretzels stay with me year after year. He proposed to me, got down on one knee by the accordion player who was playing something beautiful. The name escapes me but I still remember the notes. Karl took my hand and asked. It was that simple, the only complication was my parents, my family, and a dynasty beyond them.'

I take a sip of tea from an ornate china teacup. 'How did you meet him?'

Her eyes look distant. There's a flicker of sadness. 'He came to visit my father. My father was a relation of the Empress Elizabeth.'

I set my cup down on the saucer, trying not to break it as it lands with a crash. 'You're related to the Hapsburgs?'

'Yes,' she says, 'but I was cast out of the family when Karl and I eloped.

'That's a bold move, Maria.'

'He came one night to see Father about something, I was never told the details, and he looked at me as he left. We crossed paths in the entrance hall. When he came again the following week he handed me a note.'

'What did it say?'

'I read it later in the privacy of my room. He asked to

meet me by the concert house. He knew I loved music because he'd asked about me.'

'That would have been a risk for him,' I say.

'Yes, but he was interested in what I liked, not just in how I looked or my connections.' Her features are still striking. It isn't difficult to imagine a raven-haired beauty with the features of an Egyptian goddess - high cheekbones and dark, captivating eyes which still hold intrigue though now more cloudy. 'I decided that I wanted a future with him and if it meant leaving my family behind, so be it. I have no regrets.' She looks straight at me, her expression resolute and determined.

I am still puzzled as to why I'm here and who sent me, but her story is interesting. She hands me a note, gets up and clears away.

'I'll get going, then, I say,' taking my cue. 'Thank you. I've enjoyed talking to you.'

She nods. I tuck the note into my pocket and leave, heading back towards the tram. The sun is stronger than when I arrived and Schönbrunner Schlosstrasse is filling up with tourists as they pour out of oversized coaches. I wish they'd limit the numbers. It feels claustrophobic and they're in my way. I slip between them and down into the underground. I'm the only person who seems to know where they're going and I need to get to the first lecture of the week. It doesn't look good if you're late. I'm never late, not for anything. A train arrives as I reach the lower step. I jump on and pull the note out of my pocket, then catch myself and put it back to read later. In private. Careless risks and mistakes are dangerous and I must stay vigilant. And careful. No one is that good, not even me, and there are eyes everywhere in this city, everywhere.

Chapter 7

I open the letter in the quiet of the apartment after my lecture on the Modernists. I didn't take much of it in, but I scribbled some notes and I'll read them later. I mostly doodled sketches of landscapes and sunflowers and watched the sun disappear and reappear until it vanished completely.

Liesl,

Go to the Dorotheum auction house tomorrow at noon. There will be an auction for the New Horse Guards on the first floor. Wait until it's finished and make sure the cameras are off before you arrive. You know what to do. Wait for the next move.

I reach the Dorotheum auction house the next day well before noon as the sun begins to catch the edges of the buildings. I look up and the street is a forest of turrets and spires, the church, the buildings, all illuminated by its rays. The city is a gallery of shapes and sculptures waiting to be seen by those who will stop and look skywards towards the Gods to appreciate its beauty. I am biased, but I've seen Paris, Milan, Prague and Rome. Vienna on a warm day is unrivalled. I take a deep breath, and enter through the front doors. The red carpet and spiral stone staircase to the right give it an air of regal sophistication. With over seven hundred auctions a year, this is a busy place, and is one of the oldest and largest auction houses in the world. They have representatives in Munich, Dusseldorf, Milan, Rome, London, Prague and Brussels. I'm mindful of the links which may be useful in time. Founded by Emperor Franz Joseph in 1707, the Dorotheum is nestled within a city that is full of Hapsburg dynasty history. I imagine ladies and gentlemen from Viennese high society socialising and buying works of art. I'd love to have been a fly on the wall, listening to the hammer fall, watching the expression on their faces, feeling the adrenaline levels rising.

I scan the entrance. There are few people about. One of the guards surveys me, begins with my boots, then up to my knees and scans my black dress, settles on my eyes. He turns away but looks back as I walk towards the staircase. He won't know I've noticed.

A rare stamp collection auction will begin at ten o'clock and an antique radio auction at two. The guard is still watching. I feel his gaze as I walk up the stairs and into the main room. Priceless works of art hang on the walls. Some are placed further up in the balcony of the gallery behind wrought iron railings. The whole space is reminiscent of a ballroom, much like the ones in the Hofburg Palace. I take the stairs up to the next level. There it is, a beauty of a painting, hanging solo on a red wall, with the following words inscribed on a plaque beneath:

New Horse Guards from St. James' Park, Canaletto.
1753.
Expected to fetch ten million euros at auction.

I stop and place a hand on my chest, as though I've just seen a loved one in an open casket. It's oil on panel. This will make it much more difficult to remove than a canvas, but I can see a way around it. Johann told me it was expected to fetch more. He is one of the museum guards but he also works with us. He's useful. I know from other sources that the painting is worth at least twelve. It's not as much as the Van Gogh I deposited in the library last week, but enough for the buyer to commission its removal. I don't like to use the word *theft*. It's distasteful. I transfer pieces to homes of those who will appreciate them. To some, an art collection is not so much about the money as it is an appreciation of the quality of the artist's work. I never know who the recipients are and I treat each painting with care. Every minute of the operation gives me a thrill I've yet to find anywhere else.

I step closer to the painting and I see the Horse Guards and Downing Street, notice the rug being aired in the street, see the swirls left behind from a brush stroke. It's a work of genius. Canaletto only painted forty pieces during his ten years in London, making this item a rare treasure. His scenes of Venice are more prolific, but these were uniquely commissioned by aristocratic families for a specific purpose. My job is to lift this for a future owner.

I scan the room for cameras and guards. The power's out in this room. My technical partner, Fritz, has cut the camera and distracted the guard while I'm on this floor. I remove the painting from the wall, cut it from the frame, pull out the copy from my bag, unroll the canvas and clamp it in place. From a distance, it's difficult for the untrained eye to tell the difference between panel and canvas.

Having studied their movements for months, I have exactly two minutes to move the panel before a guard returns. They think I'm a keen buyer, and why would I be anything else? The room is quiet. I slide the painting down behind a Victorian writing bureau with dark wood panelling, large enough to conceal it for now. I take a deep breath and survey the copy on the wall as a couple wanders into the room. If anybody had walked in during the replacement, it would have looked like maintenance work, too obvious to be a theft. When I worked in Peek and Cloppenburg as a student, during the security training, we were shown a customer loading up a basket with designer Boss and Armani suits, lingering over each section, then walking out through the front doors without paying. The staff, we were told, didn't look twice, thinking the man was a window dresser. The art of a good removal is to either do it swiftly in that lucky moment when no one is around, or to be insanely obvious and appear nonchalant enough for no one to suspect that you are, in fact, a removal artist. A guard would have been a different matter, but I've calculated enough time.

Johann walks back into the room. 'Stunning detail, don't you think?'

'Hmm? Yes. It's one of my favourites.'

'You've seen the others?' he says.

'Yes, of course, although most of the best pieces are in private collections.'

He raises his eyebrows. I walk across the room to look at the rest of the antique furniture on display, draw a breath, and wait for another couple to leave the room. Johann has followed me and I feel the lightness of his breath across the back of my neck.

'A drink? Thursday evening?' he says.

'Yes,' I turn to face him. 'Why not? How about the bar on the river?'

'I'll meet you at half seven. They do food. Perhaps we can book a table.'

'Good,' I say, and I turn around, half expecting Hans to enter the gallery room.

Johann walks through into the next room, follows the couple, then stands behind them and nods in the direction of the bureau. I wait again until the room is quiet. I have four minutes before the next guard will walk in and Johann has one exit covered. By then, the job will be done, this stage of it, at least. There's an elderly man who has walked a few circuits. He seems fascinated by the still life oils on the opposite wall. They're not to my taste, but he is savouring each one. His posture is bent. I imagine years of work have curved his spine, the weight of a long life shrinking him to this size. He has a kind face and half-moon glasses. He's alone and I wonder if he has a partner. My family has been absent for so long that I'm defined only by art, my jobs, and by a need to collect things. And to appreciate beauty.

Johann is standing, motionless, by the archway through to the next room. The hunched man turns and walks away. There is no one else in sight, until a school group arrives. I now have exactly two and a half minutes. An extra guard has entered the room, possibly to watch the school party. I wait for the next break. Children are a strange breed, bouncing and giggling, flicking things at one another, ignoring rules. I envy their freedom. You should grow out of this at some point, but some never do.

I need to get the painting out from behind the bureau. I turn towards the exit and wait. The arches above me frame the edges of each room, inviting visitors into a new collection. These rooms are the kind that make you feel scruffy, uninvited, an intruder. The sense of time and of history seeps through the corridors until you're drawn deeper into the building, a palace of treasures. I shudder when I think of my next move but know I can't leave until I've moved the painting. The room is empty. I walk back to the bureau, checking each entrance again. Johann goes back into the room behind me and watches in silence. I know my time is now a fraction longer, from the timing of the last guard to exit the room. I have five minutes. I'm relying on the cameras remaining dead. I pull out a small electric screwdriver, my most useful tool. It's silent. I move towards the air ventilation system, unscrew the front panel and leave it in place. The Canaletto painting is four paces away. I pull the painting out from behind the bureau, remove the front panel of the shaft and slide the painting inside. I know it's an adequate size. I check everything first. It rests against one wall. I notice an envelope taped inside. I assume it's for me and peel it away, slip it into my inside pocket to read later. I replace the front panel and screw it back into place. This manoeuvre has taken four minutes. I move towards a gold statue, taking care not to rush out. I leave just before the next guard arrives. I walk down the staircase, admiring the surrounding walls and exhibits and will be out of the building before the antique radio auction begins, at which point, the place will be teaming with potential buyers. The new canvas painting will not be noticed by a soul. I sense someone close behind, and turn, but the staircase is empty. I reach the front entrance and leave the building.

Chapter 8

Johann has left the window ajar on the first floor by the air ventilation shaft where the Canaletto is located. I arrive with Johann and Fritz. Fritz rewired the system as I left the building. I wonder whether Fritz and Johann somehow know each other, but I'm not sure why this thought enters my mind. The road is silent. The buildings stand tall against the darkness of the evening. We are alone. The van, a charcoal grey, should not stand out. We leave it around the corner and take a hold-all with a length of rope, a cloth sheet and a screwdriver.

We reach the part of the wall below the open window, and Fritz links the hook to the rope. He throws it up and it latches to the window frame. I'm lighter and more agile, so I climb up first. Fritz follows. Johann stays on the ground. This way, if we're caught in the building he can't be linked to the crime. My hands are unusually clammy, making it difficult to grip the rope. I pull one hand up and over the other until I reach the window. I manage to pull myself up towards the frame and, with a hard tug, I'm in. Fritz has almost reached the window. His mop of red hair is tucked safely under a black beanie. Johann surveys the street for signs of life. My heart quickens and gathers pace like a horse readying itself for the beginning of the race, waiting for a gunshot.

I reach down over the window ledge to grab Fritz's hand

and haul him up into the building. After a few more tugs with both hands, he lands next to me. He shakes out his top and stands up. I should unscrew the vent, but he takes the bag, reaches down, unzips it and pulls out the screwdriver. He frees the panel across the ventilation shaft and pulls out the panel painting and I wonder who would have done the job faster. I think he may have been quicker than me by a few seconds, but I decide not to say anything.

I take a step towards the window, signal to Johann that we have removed the painting, and move away out of sight as a couple approaches. He asks them the time. I pulled the rope up and closed the window as we entered the gallery. I can't afford to make any careless moves. I remember the words in Albert's last note and my anxiety rises. The voices fade and the footsteps disappear. I press my face against the window, wait until I can see that they have gone, then open it. Fritz has tied the rope around the painting with the death grip of a snake, but it's not yet safe to lower it down to Johann. My pulse is still higher than it should be and we hear a car approach at street level. Lights fill the room and vanish, snatching away the last shadow by the pillar on the other side of the room. We hold our breath. Fritz is the first to open the window. We lift the painting carefully and push it out sideways. With a manoeuvre like this, there is always a risk of damage, but Fritz has wrapped it in cloth before tying the rope. We slide it down the outside wall until it reaches Johann on the pavement. He unties it and goes straight to the van. I look at Fritz to calm my nerves but there's still the descent. I go first, gripping the rope tightly on the way down to the street. Fritz wastes no time and is immediately above me. As his feet hit the pavement, I swing the rope out to dislodge the hook but it appears to be wedged in the window. Fritz grabs it from my fingers and yanks it hard. This time, it loosens and drops to the ground a few feet from where we are standing. He has pulled the window shut before his descent. Fritz will lock it properly early tomorrow morning and rewire the cameras. It will look as though the alarms have been turned off ready for opening.

I gather up the rope and we climb into the van. The moon outlines Johann's silhouette in the front seat. I breathe a sigh as we pull away into the darkness. The street lights are off at this time of night. A police car closes in behind us and I hold my breath. Neither Fritz or Johann move. It pulls out, passes and overtakes us. We avoid the gaze of the officers and I pray they'll continue on through the street. I don't usually pray outside the walls of the cathedral.

'We made it!' Johann turns to congratulate us.

'We haven't lifted it out of the van yet,' I say.

'Well, it's out of the building. The hard part is over,' he says.

As we pass the antique shops on the way through the city, I can't help wondering if we'll be caught before we can offload the painting. I think back to the letter and the star brooch, and know that with every move, with each new job, I risk the same fate. He should have been alive. With Albert, nothing is explained, you follow instructions to the letter. No whys, no hows, no questions asked. He rules the operations from who knows where? It could be an island in the Caribbean. Nobody asks. The van nears a bend in the road and I see the word *Polizei* in reverse letters in the wing mirror. I can't see whether it's the same patrol car that just passed us. A sense of guilt lingers, like swirls of smoke in a bar, it clings to you, leaving traces on your clothes.

'We were lucky,' says Fritz.

'Yes,' I say, but luck doesn't come into it. It's skill.

'I thought we were finished when the car drove past while you were both still in there. Gave me the jitters.' says Johann. He shuffles back against his seat.

'You can't think like that,' I say.

'Back to base and onwards,' he says, glancing at me in the mirror. I smile and look out of the window.

'I don't think they suspected anything. Probably just a routine patrol,' I say. Jobs like these tend to go wrong towards the end and it's usually down to carelessness. 'I hope that's the last time we see them.' I grit my teeth, my gaze fixed on the streets outside the window. Albert only ever gives us partial instructions. No one is ever told the whole plan. It is safer that way.

Chapter 9

A violent thunderstorm forces me to run from the tram this morning, cutting my journey time to the library in half. The damp air brings with it the scent of trees and blossom. It is difficult to see the path in front when your head is almost completely submerged under the hood of a raincoat. Every so often I peel it back and peer down to see beyond my toes and the cobbles of the pavement. A few other faces are also hidden from view under coats and umbrellas. My bag is waterproof and holds a small Van Gogh, a still life of sunflowers. It reminds me of the larger one in Amsterdam's Van Gogh Gallery but there's something appealing about a more compact work that I admire – tighter brush strokes and a composition designed with the final painting in mind. I try to imagine what the artist might have been thinking as he positioned himself to begin: a blank canvas ahead, a palette knife or a large brush in hand, maybe a cold coffee on a table somewhere out of the way. The note from the Dorotheum has led me here.

I recognise the figure walking towards me, the wide gait, almost a swagger, the height and facial features, the stubble. I know we've crossed paths before. Not here at the entrance of the library, but inside a gallery or while I've been with Hans. As he passes, I feel the hairs on the back of my neck stand on end. I turn, briefly, to check that the figure has gone and head into the library.

The instructions this time are to go to the eighteenth-century historical manuscripts. I walk past the globes, stopping to admire them for a moment. The eighteenth-century manuscripts contain some rare treasures and my body tingles at the thought of the pricelessness of the artefacts and the fact that the general public can stand so close. It feels different to standing next to a valuable painting. Something about the words and the time that they were written gives an insight into where we are today. I should take up a job lifting manuscripts, not paintings, but demand dictates the jobs and paintings are more highly sought after. I'm a small cog in a large machine. If one cog refuses to turn or removes itself, the whole system grinds to a halt. Leaving is not an option, but the thought occasionally enters my mind after a close shave or when I'm tired.

I wait for a few moments until there are no more people within view, remove volume ten and replace it with the fake Van Gogh from my bag. As I lift out the original volume, I see a newer looking piece of paper protruding from the pages. I'll look at it later. I leave the building without passing anyone on my way to the exit.

The journey back to the apartment is quick and I think about the figure passing me in the street and the note in the book. I can't risk reading it on the tram. I have a strong sense that I'm being followed and that my messages are being intercepted. Who would know about the dead drop, apart from Albert or the person who sets up the location? I doubt it's Albert who writes the notes. He's probably smoking a pipe on a chartered yacht off the coast of Monaco. Sounds like a stereotype, but that's what I picture. He would have the more glamorous end of the deal but I wouldn't swap that for the thrill of being able to touch and remove the paintings myself. The adrenaline rush is unmatched.

I jump off the tram and walk up to my building. I put the largest of the three keys in the lock, kick past the junk mail on the floor and open my mailbox on the wall with the smallest key. It's empty. I want to stand behind the doors and ambush the junk mail delivery guys as they arrive, but I'm out of the building before they reach our door and before anyone else leaves. An early start is the only way to get the work done.

Climbing the cold stone spiral staircase to the second floor, I hear echoes of footsteps several floors above. I reach my own front door, use the third key and notice that I only turn it once before the door pops open. I always lock it with two turns. Maybe I forgot this morning. I got up ten minutes late, but I never forget things. My stomach twists. Has someone been in my apartment? Why would anyone break in without busting the lock? No one has a key and if you used a skeleton key it would be impossible to lock the door behind you. I stand for a moment, my feet frozen to the mat, before taking off my shoes. I grab a large kitchen knife.

I look in the bedroom, then the living room. Nothing has been touched. I check the kitchen again and, finally, the bathroom. I kick the door back. It swings hard against the wall and stops with a bang. The shower curtain is drawn shut. I usually leave it to dry out before tucking it back into a loop against the mirror. I know I need to look behind the curtain but I hesitate. My toothbrush is on the floor. I never leave anything on the floor. As a child, I couldn't go to bed until the floor was clear. I was the unusual teenage tidy freak. I don't bend down to pick it up in case there is an intruder behind the curtain. The evening light is too low to show a silhouette.

I clutch the knife and rip the curtain back. Nothing, nobody, no belongings. Just my bath and a selection of Weleda shower gels and a shower hat. I don't like to get my hair wet, not unless I wash it.

I turn to put the knife back in the kitchen. The bedroom window is ajar. I notice as I pass the door, and return to look more closely. I never leave the window open. Two floors may be high up but I don't take that risk, and it might rain. I try to recall my movements this morning and wonder if I left in too much of a hurry to worry about the toothbrush, the window and the lock. I'm not that careless. I should let it go. There's no sign that anything has been tampered with or taken.

I go back into the kitchen, return the knife to the magnetic runner and pour myself a vodka. I reach up on tip toes to open the small built-in freezer compartment of the fridge and pull out some ice cubes. I don't cook so there's no point in having a separate freezer. I often skip meals or pick up sushi or a stir fry on the way home. I grab a smaller knife and a fresh lime from the fruit bowl and slash it in half. I cut off a slice from the middle, toss it into the glass and squeeze in some of the juice, leaving the flesh pulverised. I place the other half into a glass ramekin dish and slide it on to the top shelf of the fridge. I grab a packet of spicy crisps with the glass and take them through to the living room, setting them down on a low glass coffee table. I glance at the worn leather sofa and the urge to slump into the corner by the cushions is overwhelming, but I have to get the book from the bag in the hallway. I scrutinise the lock on the door and wonder how easy it would be to break in, then leave, half locking a door behind you. It's not the mark of a careful worker. The evidence left behind is too obvious.

I remember the figure passing me outside the library. Was it Hans? Or Albert? I've never met Albert. Maybe it was Herr Schneider, or an undercover officer. The ones who followed me from the cathedral were uniformed, making it less likely that it was planned. Maybe I was in the wrong place at the wrong time. They have a radar for things out of place.

I clutch my chest, lower my shoulders and roll my head to loosen my muscles. The weight of the bag on one shoulder, and the tension of the job, leaves me feeling tight. I'll have a hot soak later with a book and another glass of something. I reach down to the bag, lying limp on the floor next to my boots, slowly unzip it and pull out the cloth covered book. I lift it up and take it to the living room. The phone rings. I pick up the receiver but there's nobody there. I go to the window, scan the road below and the windows across the street, then draw the curtains before turning on the lamps. I slump down into the corner of the sofa, curling my feet up under me, and take a long swig of vodka. The liquid warms my insides. I untie my hair and shake out the dust and stress of the day. It's almost the weekend. I'll have to work at Cafe Heiner tomorrow, but the most demanding part of the week is over.

I set the glass down, the ice clinking against the sides, and pick up the manuscript. The cloth unravels and drops to the floor. I hold the book in the palm of my hand, run my left hand across its surface, lift it towards my nose and breathe in the smell of ageing paper, the scent of history. The feeling is thrilling. Holding an artefact this valuable in my hands makes me cling to it a few moments longer. I reach for the piece of paper from the library and tug until it's freed from the pages of the book.

The note is typed, always.

Liesl,

Do not trust Albert. You are not safe. Complete the next job then flee Vienna. He is planning to remove you. Lock your door with a dead bolt before you go to sleep. There is one more location and then you must leave the city: Akademiestrasse 21/10a.

I clutch the note with both hands and reread it, hoping I've misread the words. Why would he remove me? I'm reliable. Who wrote the note? Was it the figure who passed me today? Were they waiting to check that I went into the library? Was it written by the same person who forgot to properly lock my door? The person who knocked my toothbrush to the ground? The person who left via the bedroom window? What were they doing in my room?

I slide the note under the book and take another swig of vodka. Tipping my head back, I drain the glass.

Chapter 10

Clutching the note in a clammy fist, I walk across Museums Quarter towards the Leopold Gallery. I need to check the Leopold first, prepare for another job. The enclave of buildings are a sun trap in the hotter months with upturned giant blocks scattered across the courtyard for people to stretch out and soak up the heat like cats on a roof. In the winter months, they are used to build an ice bar. The fountains and pool are now uncovered. Boards removed from the winter months reveal a blue, green pool of shallow water. Children dabble around the edges, watch the copper coins thrown in by people passing by, those who hope for good luck. There is no such thing as luck in my line of work. You need skill. I've never understood the compulsion to throw money into water. I believe in superstitions but not the kind that cause you to part with money.

The white cube-shaped building ahead sits like a fortress, clad in white shell limestone from the Danube. It boasts a poster of Schiele's work: A contorted body, painted with an exuberance of brush strokes and palette knives. I'm not partial to a Schiele but I understand the allure. I prefer neater work with greater precision. A girl screams as she is splashed with water by another child, possibly a sibling. The concrete block behind me is the Modern Art Museum, but I prefer the Leopold, home to some of the most wanted paintings in the world.

I reach the entrance, climb the steps to my right and lean over the wall. The view allows you to scan the whole courtyard. I feel the heat of the sun against my flesh and close my eyes; the dots of people scattered across the forecourt blur as my eyelids close. The last snapshot I see is a Lowry painting – dashes of people across a canvas. I imagine them as ants scurrying across the floor to reach a hole in the ground, escaping a large cat.

A cloud passes, the light dims and the warmth retreats. I open my eyes and turn to walk up the last few steps. The entrance is a vast expanse of space with no real detail, only the woman at the ticket counter and a sparse collection of advertisements for future exhibitions. It lacks the grandeur of the Albertina, the gallery wing of the Hofburg Palace complex, but it's perfect for art. It reminds me of London's Tate Modern, but younger and less quirky.

I wind my way up the stone staircase, glancing across at the open, empty space of the entrance hall. The corridors ahead repeat themselves like a hall of mirrors. I head up towards the third floor, home to the largest Schiele collection in the world: a treasure trove of dark and twisted paintings. They lure you in and spit you out. Some of the contorted nudes are grotesque, but they are still in surprisingly high demand. I'm here to assess and to return later for a job. When I'm not moving paintings or working here, I like to look at the brighter collections, the sculptures and the Picassos.

My favourite collections are outside Vienna: Rodin's sculptures in Paris with his bronze masterpiece, *The Thinker*, and Henry Moore's collection in the Art Gallery of Ontario with the stone sculpture, *The Shape of Anxiety* – the form reminds me of a heart, held in the palm of a hand. There's also a painting I've not yet seen but I imagine it to be exquisite: da Vinci's wall mural of *The Last Supper* in the Sant Maria delle Grazie. I've been to Milan, but I was working. I will have to return.

I scan the rooms that I need to see, then leave and head to Akademiestrasse, following the instructions on the note. It's on the opposite side of Kärntner Strasse to the Opera House, tucked away behind the shops. I decide to walk instead of going by tram. It's not far and I will cut through the Burggarten. The blooms are in full explosion in May. I stride past the small Romanesque amphitheatre and the café selling ice cream and coffee. It's a shell of a place in the winter, boarded up and closed for business. I watch a small boy weaving his way through the rose beds hiding from a young girl. A woman is walking alongside with a pram, the top of a wrapped bundle just visible.

I pass children playing in the sand pit and, as the trees open up to a view of the Hofburg Palace at Heldenplatz, there appears to be a beer festival with wooden huts and women wearing dirndls and men in lederhosen serving Bavarian specialties. Someone offers me a beer. It's tempting but I wave an arm and keep moving. I reach Akademiestrasse and search the numbers for 21a. I ring the bell to apartment 10a and wait. It's an unusual request. My stomach twists and I'm carrying a gun, just in case. This is neither a job or a drop off. A man answers but gives no name.

'Who is it?' Asks the voice from the buzzer.

'Liesl,' I say, turning my head to speak into the small microphone.

A selection of family names runs down alongside two rows: Moritz, Friedlander, Schulz, Fritzl, Weiser, Bittenauer.

'Come up,' says a voice.

I don't recognise it and I hear another voice but put it down to interference. I push the door open with a click. It feels heavier than most apartment front doors. Paint is peeling in chunks of green faded gloss. I look at the lift and decide, instead, to use the stairs. The stone staircase winds up to four more floors of apartments. Black swirls of wrought iron railings curl up towards the roof. They don't look high enough, given the drop down through the centre of the stairwell. I continue up to the third floor. Number 9 is to my far right. 10A is straight ahead, the left of the two doors. I lean in to press the buzzer but the door is opened by a short man in a suit before my finger reaches the button. He looks at me without a word, doesn't open the door fully and peers over my shoulder before stepping back to let me in. He closes the door behind me. I'm not sure who he's expecting, but I've come alone.

'Can I ask your name?' I ask, as he studies me.

'Albert,' he says. I feel a chill. He doesn't fit the image I had in my mind. I can't picture this small frame of a man rubbing shoulders with criminal gang leaders. He looks more like a banker or an upmarket salesman. His gaze is unnerving. I don't know why I'm here and we've never met. I don't like to be unprepared and my throat tightens, stifling my voice. It cracks as I ask what he wants.

'Sit down, Liesl. I'd like to talk.' He flicks his hand towards the sofa in the living room and I position myself on the edge. I can feel him watching me but when I turn, he looks away and out of the window.

'Coffee?' he asks.

'Yes. Black.'

Without any acknowledgement he disappears from the room. Klimt sketches line the walls. They are from the same series as the ones owned by Herr Schneider, but this would not be obvious to the untrained eye. I wonder how well they know each other. An array of bronze sculptures and porcelain figurines line windows and tables. There are a few oil paintings on the walls, nothing significant. I imagine he owns a safe for more valuable works. I've worked for him for three years but I know nothing, other than his first name and the jobs he contracts out.

I hear a phone in another room. He answers. Muffled words are cut short as he hangs up. The scent of fresh coffee and the sounds of bubbling water come from the kitchen. There's something unusual about the apartment, but I can't say what. He re-enters with one coffee.

'Are you not going to have some?' I ask. He ignores my question, hands me a small cup on a saucer and remains standing.

'Liesl, you've done your job well. You're quick, discrete and reliable.' I wonder whether he is building up to firing me, or worse. 'But I don't have any use for you any more. I'd like you to see Herr Schneider before we wrap up.'

There is a bang outside. I jump, then realise that it's the absence of sound that makes the apartment feel odd. There's no sound from the street below, despite buses, cars or people passing. I feel panic rising and I wonder if it was Albert, or one of his employees, who entered my apartment. I must have forgotten to lock it. I'll add the dead bolt later. I'm not a careless person. I never forget anything and I don't leave things on the floor. Albert stands with one hand in his pocket.

'Go over to the painting on the wall,' he says, pointing at the Cézanne..

I put the coffee down and stand up slowly, careful to keep my breathing in check. Never show fear. Animals can smell fear and so, too, can humans. Albert watches as I move. I walk over to the painting behind the sofa: a still life arrangement of fruit, scattered across a table, a dark background with an unseen light source illuminating a white cloth. For a moment all I can see is the darkness and my eyes rest on a skull to one side. It's a Cézanne, but not an original. I suspect the original is somewhere out of sight.

'What is it that you want?' I ask, but I don't turn to face him. If he has no use for me anymore, a note would have been enough. We don't need to meet now. I realise he wants to get rid of me. I'd managed to convince myself that the note was a diversion.

I hear a shot then the thud of a body and the metallic clatter of a gun falling. I drop to the floor behind the sofa, but there is no sound or movement. I wait for a few seconds, then stand to find Alfred's body slumped over the coffee table. The gun is beside him on the floor, blood is pooling on the crimson carpet. I must leave the building before somebody calls the police. I hear a creak behind me and, instead of looking around, I run towards the front door. My feet pummel the steps until I reach ground level. I hear the main front door slam and I hide in a passage where the bins are stored. I hear footsteps walking towards me and up the staircase. I crouch and wait, trying to control my breathing.

I should walk out of the building at a normal pace but I almost break into a run as I reach the door. Pearls of sweat form on my forehead and my heart is beating right up into my skull. I walk down the street towards the ring, picking up my pace. I drop a glove and deliberate over whether or not to go back for it. A man has picked it up and is standing holding it. I stand still as the number 1 tram pulls up outside the Bristol Hotel. I jump on, breathless, almost falling into the seat for the elderly or disabled. As I look out of the window, I see the figure that I could swear I saw outside the library on the day I deposited the Van Gogh. The tram doors slam shut. I wait for it to pull away and until the figure is out of sight, then walk toward the back where the seats are usually empty. I sit in the corner, facing forwards, clutching my bag.

A suicide doesn't seem plausible unless the other voice on the intercom wasn't interference. Was there somebody else in the room? It would have been a difficult shot from either of the two doors into the living room. Why is he sending me to Schneider? Had he planned to kill me and changed his mind at the last moment? Has he ordered Schneider to do it instead?

I've never met Albert. How do I know if it was him? I am not sure who to trust, who followed me, who broke into my apartment and who wrote the note? Could the same person have been involved in all of these incidents? The more I think about it, the less anything makes sense. Back at the apartment, I find an envelope in my letterbox from Maria, asking me to visit her tomorrow. I need to fit a deadlock.

Chapter 11

I step off the number 38 tram a stop before Herr Schneider's house. Albert's words make my blood run cold. Is Schneider going to finish the job? My legs ache and I haven't slept for a whole night since the shooting at Albert's apartment, despite fitting a deadlock the following day. I suspect the apartment doesn't belong to him.

The bell on the tram rings with a shrill warning as a pedestrian courageously crosses the tracks. People gamble with traffic at their peril in this city. I used to try, until I was almost knocked down by a lorry. The sense of danger and rebellion as I crossed the tram lines was abruptly curtailed as I stumbled into the car lane with the Do Not Cross sign. I can still remember the screeching of the brakes and the driver furiously waving his arm at me. He managed to stop two feet short of my boots as I looked up through his window.

An elderly lady is battling with her walking stick and shopping trolley, and I get up before my stop to help her. As I hold the stick and take her arm, she smiles at me with a look of surrender.

'Danke schön,' she says. Her voice reminds me of Maria's. Sometimes they refuse, but I always offer. If Omama was still alive, I'd want others to do the same. I clutch my bag and climb down the steps after they open out and down. The curb is a steep drop. I turn back to help the lady with the stick but she is gone. It's late morning and Herr Schneider's curtains are closed. I open the gate, walk up the path and ring the bell three times. I wait longer this time. I stand back a pace or two and see a flash of movement from an upstairs curtain. I press my ear to the door and listen as footsteps on the stairs become louder. I step back as I hear him moving along the corridor towards me. The top latch is turned. I hear a bolt flip and the turn of a key in a lock that clinks as it revolves.

The security is much tighter than most houses. I don't know any other homes with bolts. The door opens enough for me to see one eye. I remember the narcissi as I grimace and wait to see if he remembers me. He doesn't immediately appear to, but I hope that he will be able to recollect our discussion about Klimt and other artists.

'Liesl?' he asks, as though he is not expecting me.

'Yes.' I nod and wait.

He opens the door a little wider. 'Come in.' His voice is as brusque as it was on my previous visit but with an impatience that keeps me from stepping inside. He pulls the door wider and walks off in the direction of the study. This time, he omits the offer of coffee and I'm relieved. I don't want to stay any longer than is necessary. He goes to the drawer of his desk and pulls out an envelope. I stand in the doorway of the study opposite the living room and scan the walls. Several African prints hang amongst sketches and oils – an eclectic mix of pictures from around the world, nothing special.

He hands me an envelope and waits. I wonder why I'm here, given that Albert is no longer alive. It occurs to me that he may have another worker who's unaware that I've been dismissed. Does Albert's death make my dismissal void? Am

I still being assigned jobs? Herr Schneider walks out of the room. My eyes follow him into the living room and I watch him settle in his armchair. This must be the one that he usually sits in because there's a dent in the seat, and he sat in the same one last time I visited. It faces the window, looking out on passing trams and the houses opposite. I enter the room and sit on the opposite chair with my back to the window, but close enough to the front door. He nods again.

I run my finger along the seal of the envelope, catching the edge of the paper. I notice blood where the envelope has cut through the skin under the index finger of my right hand. I realise I shouldn't have opened it, not here. Herr Schneider stands up, takes the envelope, closes it and leads me towards the front door. I don't ask for a tissue and move swiftly out of the room into the hallway. He gives me a fabric handkerchief with the initials *FHJS* embroidered in one corner with heavy gold thread. I feel a shred of guilt as my blood stains his perfectly white, ironed handkerchief. He hands back the letter, opens the door, then closes it firmly behind me.

I wait for the tram back into town, holding the handkerchief around the wound until it stops throbbing. It's a deeper cut than a usual paper cut. I've never needed to stem the flow of blood and I wonder why the paper is so sharp at the edges. The red and white metal front of the 38 tram rises over the brow of the hill and a sense of relief washes over me. It feels safer as soon as I leave the scene: the library, a gallery, Herr. Schneider's house. Although, I never know how safe I am in any given situation, from security guards, from the police, and now from any of Albert's co-workers. The tram grinds to a halt and the steps move out and down towards the pavement, reminding me of the stabilisers I had on my bicycle as a child. I climb up and find a seat. There are none at the back, so I move towards the front. I find a double set of empty seats and sit by the window. Pulling the note out from my bag, I open it and I catch my breath as I see the name at the bottom.

Dear Liesl,

I have a job for you to do. I want you to go to the library at noon tomorrow. Deposit the Schiele and you'll find the next assignment.

Albert

I fold the note in a hurry and push it down into my bag along with the horror of the fact that he is still alive. I assumed, when Herr Schneider handed me the note, that it was from someone else. I can't fathom how Albert can possibly be alive, although I didn't wait around to check his pulse before I left the apartment.

I feel faint. I don't know if my apartment is safe or where I should go if it isn't. The Art now appears to be in the wrong hands. I can't let this slip through my fingers, not yet. Maria's words still haunt me. The walls are closing in and I can't figure out what to do. Albert is not to be trusted.

The tram judders as it crosses the tracks and veers off to the right, before ploughing under the arches of the rail tracks above and on into the city. I look out of the window, the traffic on the ring going on for miles. Dusk is a curious time of day, the lights dazzle and the reds across the skyline are ominous in their promise of tomorrow's sunlight. The gap between day and night brings a fearful mix of colours.

Chapter 12

I knock on Maria's door. She opens it slowly. 'Maria? Everything all right?' I ask.

'Yes.' she says, 'Come in.' She ushers me into the living room where tea is already laid out on the coffee table in china cups. These are different, more ornate. She looks pale and tired.

'Why do you need to see me?' I ask.

'There are things I need to tell you,' she says, nodding in the direction of the armchair where I usually sit. 'Please, sit.'

Nothing makes sense – the gun, the warning note, the lock on the door of the apartment, Albert. *Albert.* His name refuses to leave my mind: An imposter.

'Go on,' I say.

'Tea?' she asks, already pouring me a cup. 'Liesl, how well do you know Hans?'

'Hans? I'm not sure I understand.'

'Yes. You do,' she says. 'You must have suspected.'

'Suspected what? Do you know him?'

'Liesl, he came to see me.'

'You don't suspect he has been part of Albert's … circus?'

The image of Albert makes me tense and my anger rises. Knowing now that Hans has been in Maria's home, I realise Albert may not be the only ringmaster.

'How does he know who you are or where you live? What does he have to do with this?' Memories of him turning up at the Dorotheum and the coffee shop, after the police tailed me, flood back.

'He's been following you, Liesl.'

'What did he say?'

'That he's been hired by an insurance firm in London.'

'Insurance firm? Which one?'

'I don't remember, Fairbrother, Fairweather, Something similar. Liesl, every move, every job has been watched. Monitored.'

This is not what I imagined she would tell me. Why would he go to see her? Does he know Albert? As my mind spirals, she pours herself a cup of tea and begins to slice the strudel. Her homemade apfelstrudel is hard to turn down. Chunks of apple, coated with sugar and cinnamon. I watch the knife slicing through apple flesh, pastry coming off in flakes as each section is crushed.

'Why would he come and see you to tell you that he is following me? It doesn't make sense. Do you think someone suspects fraudulent claims?'

'It's difficult to say. What I do think is that you are in grave danger.'

'I was given a note a while ago telling me that I should leave the apartment, but I stayed. I've fitted a deadbolt.'

Her eyes rise from the strudel. 'Who do you think sent it? Do you think it was Hans?'

'No. I don't know. Albert? Someone else? Albert asked to see me.' I decide not to tell her that he was shot. He appears to be alive. I feel nauseous. I want to know whether she thinks he is dead or alive. Trust no one.

'What did he want?' she asks.

'Difficult to say. He was cryptic.'

'That's strange. He doesn't usually see people face to face.'

'That's what I thought, but I went,' I say.

'And what happened?'

'He just thanked me for my work and gave me the next assignment.'

'That's odd,' she says, gazing out of the window.

'Maria. Do you know where he lives?'

'Yes, out in the 22nd district. Why?'

My heart sinks. The apartment I went to wasn't Albert's. If he doesn't live there, how do I know it was Albert I saw?

'What does he look like?'

'That seems a strange question, Liesl. You said yourself that you saw him.'

'Just tell me,' I say, losing patience.

'He's tall and has a limp. He has a beard and he reminds me of an Italian businessman I once knew, distinguished.'

I feel nauseous, realising the man who was shot wasn't Albert. Was Albert even there? Who fired the shot?

'Could I have some water?' I ask, hoping to calm my nerves and regain some composure.

'Yes, of course.' She gets up and goes to the kitchen. I hear the tap. If Albert is lying to me, what will happen next?

Maria returns with a full glass and I wish it was vodka. She says nothing, cuts another slice. As the knife presses into the soft centre, pieces of the pastry case rebel, falling to the sides of the plate. I think of the body strewn across the pavement, his flesh, cold. Icing sugar falls to the sides leaving a clean cross section through the apple. Maria's silence is unnerving. I stare at the slice as she hands it to me.

I should be anticipating the taste, but I'm still thinking about Hans. Was the lunch on that day premeditated? Was he just doing his research? Finding out about me and reporting back? And to whom?

'Liesl, an insurance company in London suspected illegal claims from a collector and they hired Hans who traced the paintings back to Albert and then you.'

'Did Hans say anything else to you? Anything that would help piece this together?'

'No, just that you weren't what he expected.'

'What did he expect?'

'It's difficult to say, an older person, a man perhaps. Who knows what he usually finds? I think he likes you.' I choose to ignore this last comment. Why is it surprising that I could shift these works of art? 'You're not what I expected either so I can imagine his reaction. When I first met you I wasn't sure why you had signed up to this. You have too much to lose. I'm old enough for it not to matter any more but you have your whole life ahead of you.'

'That's ridiculous,' I say. 'It doesn't matter how old you are. I'm unattached. I have no children, no parents, no friends. No one would even notice if I went missing, apart from you, the Heiner and Leopold staff and the university.'

'Liesl, the best thing you can do is pretend you know nothing and to carry on. If you know about Hans, it gives you the upper hand. Use it to your advantage. Give him snippets of information. Throw him off scent.'

'You're a smart woman, Maria. Won't he suspect something's wrong if I lead him in the wrong direction?'

'No. You'll just be making his job harder. It's what I'd do if I were in your shoes. Give him the runaround. Talk about the wrong locations, the wrong paintings.'

I need to figure out how to lose him. My priority is to find out about the body in the apartment. 'Albert's been sending me to one of his contacts, a man in the 19th,' I say.

Maria sits back on her embroidered cushion and folds her arms. 'Oh, Frans?'

'Herr Schneider?'

'Yes. Frans Schneider. His brother was meant to give you the first note and the star brooch but Albert finished him off.'

I lean in towards her. 'Brother? Albert finished him off? Am I next?'

'Possibly. You said, yourself, that you are in danger and if he tried to kill you then you're not safe. Liesl, you need to know about the works.'

'The art?'

'Yes, of course.' She remains expressionless.

I finish my tea and stay fixed on the edge of the seat. Schneider's brother, the body in the apartment, now me?

Chapter 13

She lowers her head. 'Albert has been taking art, at least ordering you to take works belonging to Jewish families in Vienna. I don't want to insult your intelligence by assuming that you're unaware of the possessions plundered during the nineteen thirties and forties.' She looks at me as though it is a question.

'You mean the Anschluss?' I know that she can't bring herself to utter the word. Her pained expression reveals some of the years of horror. I knew enough. 'Nineteen thirty-eight,' I say.

'Liesl, my mother was Jewish. She ...' Maria looks at the floor as her sentence trails off into a hollow silence. She looks up and studies my face. 'They were taken. The Gestapo arrested both of my parents and deported them to Dachau. From there they were sent to Auschwitz.' She stops, her face turning grey. There's nothing I can add that will take away the sting. The art, and Albert, now feel inconsequential and I watch her lower lip tremble as she struggles to find the words to finish her story.

'Maria, you don't have to tell me any more.' I feel powerless. It's the same sense of helplessness that I remember feeling when I was told I would not see my parents again. I can't remember their faces. I spill my tea and she jumps, only a fraction, but enough to notice. 'I'm so sorry,' I say, 'I'll get a cloth.' She is up and on her feet, moving towards the kitchen before I can put my cup down. 'What did the art have to do with Albert?' I ask, trying to change the subject.

She pauses, 'The government, the galleries – the Leopold and the Belvedere — they are holding pieces belonging to Austrian Jews. It would be scandalous if enough people knew. But therein lies the problem; nobody knows and what they don't know, as my Mother used to say, makes the issue invisible.' The word *invisible* ricochets through the air. She looks at me, as though searching for something, a response, an assurance, maybe. 'Much of the art was taken by German soldiers and used as exit permits for Jewish residents in Vienna. My aunt fled to America, expecting her belongings and her paintings to follow.' She looks away. 'It never did. After the Anschluss they took everything. It was all plundered and later changed hands, sold on to private collectors and gallery owners. Liesl, more than three million pieces are in the wrong hands.'

'I'm part of the process,' I say, feeling disgusted with Albert and with myself, but I don't think like a museum curator, I think as a thief – because this is what I am – and, like a private collector, I do not subscribe to the belief that works of art belong only in the public arena. Location is important. I was trained – primarily by Albert, and previously by a man named Hermann – to discover the location of as many pieces as possible. I studied the catalogues and auction houses with the eyes of a hawk. That way, when a job comes in I know where to begin.

'You weren't to know,' she says. But I do know, now, and this changes everything. The light intensifies, momentarily, catching her face and defining the lines and curves of her cheeks and chin. I can see, now, what I should have been able to see before: her dark, piercing eyes, the definition of her face, the books on the shelves. Her intellect, her love of literature, her interest in Jewish history. There are so many small details that I miss, but only with people. People, I find endlessly difficult to read, and this is why I prefer to be alone, to avoid being let down, to have no expectations or delayed hopes. Paintings are a different matter altogether.

'Liesl, when they took my parents I should have been with them but I was staying with a friend. I remember them hiding me in their basement when guards knocked on their door.' I don't know what to say to her, there are no words that would help her now. Her eyes glisten. 'I remember the smell of damp, musty air and the sound of heavy footsteps and muffled voices above my head. I waited for them to open the hatch and find me, but the voices went quiet and I heard a door close.' She lowers her head, then looks up at me. 'When the hatch eventually opened I didn't know who it would be, but it was Marta's face, my friend's Mother.' There was a pause and she began to play with her ring. 'I will never forget the way she squeezed me; as though she would never let me go. Then I saw her look at her husband with fear in her eyes. It was a fear that I saw in my Mother's eyes all those years before.'

'What happened?' I had read about the extermination camps. I've never forgotten the details: the hair, the shoes, the gas chambers, the photographs etched in my mind.

'When they took me home the next day, our neighbour told me they had been taken. People think that children don't see things, that they don't know. No one knows the consequences of these moments until they experience the same kind of terror. It breaks you in a way that makes it difficult to put the pieces back together. If you break again, somewhere in the future, those cracks, they are a point of weakness, a point where the process of shattering begins again.'

I sit in silence. The flicker of sadness that sometimes passes in her eyes like clouds, now makes sense.

'The house was ransacked. I didn't speak for weeks,' she continues, taking a sip of tea, as though it might steady her nerves.

'I'm so sorry,' are the only words I can find, the right words just out of reach.

'They lost everything,' she says. 'Five thousand pieces were burned in total from across Austria, from houses that were plundered.' She swallows the end of the word, as though trying to keep it from fully forming. 'And others were auctioned off to international markets.'

My heart sinks as I realise the enormity of what happened. The burning I can't take the blame for, but I've been helping to move art into international markets and have almost certainly helped deposit treasured pieces and family heirlooms into the wrong hands. My stomach twists as I watch her tears fall. 'And the recovery?' I ask.

'Very little,' she says, shaking her head, 'And most of it is in galleries and museums. Once it's sold on the black market to a gallery owner, who unwittingly purchases a looted piece, it becomes very difficult to recover. Then, there are those who think that they belong in the public domain for more people to enjoy.'

'Well, you know what I think,' I say. The question is, will they ever all be returned to their rightful owners?'

'I very much doubt it, but I can live with the hope that it may just happen,' she pauses, 'in time.'

'So, what has Albert been doing with the paintings? Where

are they all going?' It's an inevitable but necessary question.

'That's the problem. He's been taking pieces through you,' she nods in my direction, 'and selling to galleries for a higher price, posing as a private owner.' I assumed they were going to private collectors, but my job is only to lift and deposit. I've never felt like a thief, despite what I do and the circles in which I move. Now, with the knowledge of the original owners, I feel, for the first time, a sense of shame. It's not a familiar sensation. I want to go home and shower, walk away, but I need to think of a reason to leave.

'What do you think?' she asks.

'I don't know. I think we need to find a way to outsmart him. Confronting him or pulling out isn't an option.' The gravity of the situation weighs heavy on my mind. This is her story and it is the story of millions of others like her.

'I never liked him,' she says.

'Really? I say, remembering the room, the gun and the man. The deception has been subtle, covering his deeds in layers of half-truths and unanswered questions. I still don't know who tried to shoot me. I feel a chill and I turn to look out of the window. The clouds have greyed, closing in around the building. My chest feels tight and my pulse quickens. 'I don't know the identity of the ...'

'The body? she says, finishing my sentence. 'It will just be one of his minions, like you and me, my dear.'

'I'm not so sure,' I say to her, wondering whether it was the figure who passed me outside the library on that rainy day, or the person who may, or may not, have entered my apartment, knocked my toothbrush to the ground, forgotten to turn the key twice, or left the window open. I never leave windows open. You know the entry points the way you know your route to work, or your bank pin code. You notice each stop, each button. You have to know how to access your account or a building. They are all one and the same thing. One holds cash, the other art; both commodities. The difference between them is that, despite what they say about art heists, I value the pieces. I'm passionate about the work. Most art thefts are undertaken by men, or women, who are ignorant of the works and their true value. Look at the Gardener theft in Boston – the pieces were ripped from their frames with no respect for their beauty or their cultural heritage. I'd like to think that I'm different. Albert, on the other hand, has no sensitivities about art and a complete disregard for human life.

'Liesl, he's playing us all. The only reason I'm involved in this is because he threatened me. And don't forget, my dear, that you, too, are sinking deeper into criminal activity.'

She's right, I am a criminal, but it hasn't bothered me until now. It's a job and I have the skill but I must now return these pieces to their owners. Plain theft, or movement of art to order, as I see it, is very different to the looting and pillaging of precious family art. I have to act quickly, before Albert catches up with me and I'm mindful of the threat to my life, mindful of the bodies I've already encountered.

Chapter 14

I pass the odd tourist, but the city is eerily quiet. The lull in the summer, before the tourists begin to arrive in the run up to the Christmas Markets, is when I need to be more careful. There are no crowds to slip into, nowhere to hide. Tourists used to arrive in December, now the markets begin in November. They open earlier each year, and the people begin to arrive from October. In July and August, the streets are almost deserted, a ghost town of towering buildings and wide, shimmering pavements, a mirage of shapes. Those with enough sense, or money, escape to the cool of the Alps, places where there's a mountain breeze and a view. The city becomes a heat trap in the summer; the streets, humid and airless.

I hear footsteps behind me picking up speed. There are few people about and I clench my bag with the Schiele inside. I removed it some time ago. As I step up my pace, the footsteps keep pace with mine. My stomach tightens and an arm is wrapped around my neck, pulling me backwards. I hit the torso of the body behind me and am pulled in tight. I can't breathe. I hear myself gasping for air but don't let go of the bag. I begin to feel light-headed. It's a man's body – the hairs on the arm, the force of the grip. I'm experiencing the beginnings of asphyxiation. I throw my head back into his, stamp hard on his foot with my heel and swing my body to the side. Pushing the bag out of the way, I make a fist and wrench my left elbow back with the force that I need to elbow him in the stomach. I hear a muffled groan, and his grip loosens. I turn around as he's forced backwards, bent double and clutching his stomach. The power shifts, momentarily. I know I should run but I need to see his face. As his head rises, I realise we've never met. I kick his shin with a sharp jab and turn to run. He was after the painting and knew it was in my bag. His approach and attack tells me that this is an inside job.

I turn a corner, still clutching the bag, and make a sharp right turn. There are no footsteps, not a sound, but I don't stop until I'm home. As I stand outside the building and look up, something stops me from going into my apartment. There's no open window or anything suspicious, but I know in the pit of my stomach. It is a feeling I've learned not to ignore.

I decide to go back to Maria's. I'll deposit the painting another time. The question in my mind is, who would have known about the painting, other than Albert? How many people? You never know how many are in the chain. Sometimes more is better, as you can't be traced as easily, but with the larger, more valuable pieces, having less people involved is a safer way of organising an operation. This one is small, but valuable. If I was removed from the chain, it would never reach its destination. Maria once asked me why I would risk my life for these works, for him, and I don't have an answer, but a museum isn't always the best place for works of art, especially with the new knowledge that some of it is looted art. I don't blame the galleries, they wouldn't know. Sometimes, a private collector will look after a painting better. That's my personal view, but it's not a popular one.

As the train pulls in, the air is forced up the steps from the station, thick and hot. I rush down the last few steps and jump into a carriage. Beads of sweat form on my neck. This train has no air conditioning. I take a seat by an open window and tie my hair up in a knot. As the train pulls out of the station, I see a reflection of the assailant. He can't have followed me, not at that speed. I look again, carefully, into the darkened glass of the window. If I look close enough I see only blurred bricks as they whizz past and disappear into the darkness. I pull back and look at his figure, honing in on his features, and I realise that it's not him. The relief is palpable. I take a deep breath and put on a cap. I clutch the bag down to my right between my thigh and the window. The backs of my knees are damp and clammy.

I get off at Schönbrunn and notice that Maria's curtains are drawn, to shield the sitting room from the sun. I hope that's all. I ring on the bell and she looks troubled as she opens the door ajar.

'Are you all right?' I ask.

'Yes, just woken up,' she says, opening the door wider and ushering me in.

'I'll make you some tea. I don't have strudel today,' she says, and disappears off into the kitchen.

I don't mind. My stomach is still churning from the incident outside the library and I wonder whether the man on the train was the man who tried to attack me. When I looked into the window, before I got off the train, he was gone.

I place the bag down beside my chair and feel a pulsing through my arms and chest. The adrenalin is still coursing through my body, preparing me for an escape. I breathe deeply, in and out, until my heart rate slows to a normal rhythm. Maria crosses the kitchen to reach the milk in the fridge and I get up to look at her books. A photograph of a couple, I presume, her parents; a grainy, black and white picture with creases, where it might have been kept in a pocket before it would have been put into the silver, rectangular frame, sits at the front of the middle shelf. The lack of colour in black and whites draws your eyes to the shape and form of a portrait. The woman in the photo is in a separate photograph next to it, the frame, more gilded. She looks like Maria, but her face is a different shape. Both display a look of steely determination. You can see the pain in her eyes, the sadness from a life of love, loss, persecution and fear. I can't imagine what it must have been like to live through it all but I know that I must try to bring some justice. There needs to be restitution, however modest and I will do what I can, however small.

Cloth-bound encyclopaedias and several atlases are tucked away behind the photographs, along with a series on Freud and a history of psychoanalysis. His office, now a museum on Berggasse, houses his couch and artefacts from all over the world. What I wouldn't give to spend an hour with him, talking over an espresso about the mind and its quirks. To have the privilege of a glance inside his mind would bring me pleasure. There are smaller books in German and Hebrew. The Hebrew alphabet is an art form in itself. The German titles are mostly novels and nothing of interest. I don't have the time or the patience for novels. Travel books are towards the top, but she hasn't spoken about travel. The largest collection is on Art and Art History. This doesn't surprise me, but what does catch my attention is the style of art she has chosen. There are books on Rothko, Kandinsky and Warhol, and I wonder why she's interested in the Impressionists and the Renaissance, the very pieces that we remove.

She returns to the room with a tray, sets it down steadily on the coffee table, and looks over at the bookshelves. 'See anything you like?'

'Yes,' I say, 'we have similar tastes, although my fiction collection is fairly sparse.' She smiles. 'Maria, what's your interest in the art that we remove?'

She sits down, as though she hasn't heard my question or isn't going to reply. 'I wanted to work with the best.'

'The best?' I say.

'Yes, I needed to find a way of getting the art back ... to my family and to all the other families. The art that was plundered has never been returned. The injustice of it, Liesl, it's wrong.'

'I don't understand.'

'I found Albert through a friend who is an art dealer.' I feel my frown as I listen to her explanation, hoping that it will make sense. 'He told me that Albert had lifted the largest collection of works from museums across Europe and I had him followed. It led them to you and that's when I wanted to get to know you, find out how you operate and then become a part of the circuit. I needed someone with your experience and ability to help me get it back.'

'You had him followed? I didn't have you pinned as that type.'

She shrugs her shoulders. 'Well, dear, can you ever truly know people?

Chapter 15

Tonight, I have booked a table for two out on the deck of the Sky Restaurant above Steffl, with a view of the cathedral roof. I reach Kärntner Strasse and get into the lift. The doors close and I press the button for the sixth floor. The capsule moves upwards – slowly, steadily – past the mosaic on the building opposite. I reach the sixth floor and take a smaller lift to the seventh floor, the penthouse above the department store. You can take the internal lift through Steffl to the top floor until six, but after closing only the outside lift is available. I feel mildly claustrophobic in this smaller lift. As the doors close, a hand grabs one of the doors, stops it from closing completely. I jump. Hans steps in to join me.

'I saw you getting into the lift but just missed it. I followed you up.'

'Just in time,' I say. 'I booked a table outside.'

'Sounds good.'

He has dressed up. I feel scruffy in my charcoal cotton dress and regret not making more of an effort. He inspects my dress, says nothing and presses the button for the seventh floor as the doors close. We're forced to stand close together and I can smell his aftershave – a heavy musk. The doors open and we enter the restaurant, past oversized champagne bottles and a glass case of mouthwatering tortes. The waiter takes my name, nods and leads us out through a narrow door to a table on the roof terrace, with views out across the city spires and towards the hills to Kahlenburg and Leopoldsburg to the north of the city.

'Here, Madam.' He pulls out a seat for me, ignoring Hans.

'Thank you. Could we have the wine menu, please?' Hans nods and sits down opposite me. The tables are almost full and I'm glad I booked. I look out towards the cathedral. 'Beautiful, isn't it?'

He smiles and follows my gaze towards the roof tiles, as they turn a shade of burnt amber in the intensity of the low evening sunlight. It catches the rooftops, illuminating the spires and the ornate glazed tiles of the cathedral rooftop; the greens and yellows, criss-crossing in diamond shapes, reminds me of a pack of cards. The double-headed eagles of the Haspsburg dynasty look out over the city, guarding it from evil. The roof is the only part of the cathedral where snow refuses to settle in the winter, its angle too steep to hold the weight, casting the snow down towards the pavement below.

'It's good to see you, Liesl,' he says. 'I haven't seen you much in the café. It's been so busy.'

'I thought it would be good to catch up.' Maria's comments have been playing on my mind since the visit. 'It's difficult to talk in the café. How's your week been?'

'Same as usual, I go back to London for a few days next week. You'll share a bottle with me, won't you?' he asks, looking up from the wine menu.

'Yes, I prefer red.'

'OK, I'll have a steak.' he says. 'You?'

'I'll have a schnitzel,' I say, as I look out toward the hills. I feel his eyes on me. 'Hans, have you been hired to watch me?' I ask, realising this is a risky question.

'What? I don't understand.'

'Are you watching my movements?'

'Why would I want to watch what you are doing?'

'Did you break into my apartment?' I don't really expect the truth, but I need to see his response.

'No. Liesl, what are you getting at? Is everything all right?'

'Don't change the subject. I've heard a rumour that you have been hired to watch my movements and I wanted to hear it from you.'

'Well, you can hear from me that there has been nothing untoward going on.'

'That's not the question I asked. I asked if you broke into my apartment.' I feel my anger rising.

'Why would I want to do that?' His face remains expressionless, unemotional.

'Answer the question.' I hear my voice rise above the quiet mutterings from tables surrounding us. I put down my menu and place the palms of my hands flat on to the starched white tablecloth, my elbows forming two corners of a square as I brace myself. I look straight at him. He remains unruffled. I feel he's been prepared for this conversation since the moment we met in the café kitchen, if not before. He leans back and folds his arms, a physical barrier to my flow of words.

'Liesl, there's nothing to answer.'

'Nothing?'

'That's correct.'

'I have just accused you of following me and you have nothing to say?'

'Liesl, you have a vivid imagination and some rumour has created a world in your mind that just isn't true.'

'You think you can patronise me without answering a single question? I don't even know who you are. You're far too smart to be wasting your hours in a coffee shop, and you show up in the same places as me on your days off.' I can hear myself shouting the final few words. I take a deep breath and a large swig of wine. This flash of anger is rare. The waiter appeared and disappeared at some point in the conversation. I noticed when the glass was placed in front of me, deep crimson against the white tablecloth, the glint of light on the upper edge of the glass. I noticed the glare.

I fight the urge to leave the restaurant and wait for a response from Hans. I suspect I won't gain any more information. I cross my legs and look straight at him. I hope it will give him a sense of unease or, at least, a sliver of guilt or remorse. I suspect, at this point, that Maria was right. I know he won't give me the truth.

'I don't know how you've conjured up this wild idea,' he says, 'but it doesn't even make sense. Why would I follow you? What use would it be to me? We work in the café together, and I can't imagine there's more to your life outside it than your studies and a fairly quiet social life.'

I chose to ignore the last comment. I drink more wine and look out to the cathedral, noticing the shadows as the sun lowers. I look back, his position and expression remain unchanged. He gives nothing away and he does not break his gaze. I should have left by now after my outburst, but I don't want to leave empty handed..

'My source is reliable,' I say.

'Really? Are you sure?'

'I'm sure. I didn't believe it at first but then I remembered bumping into you in the café behind Graben. Well, you followed me inside.' He raises one eyebrow, a trick I still cannot master.

'Why would I follow you?' he asks, 'Give me one good reason.'

I can't, not without giving him an insight into Albert's world. Does he know? I feel torn between his convincing look of surprise and the sincerity of all that Maria has told me, unless Albert has fed the idea to Maria to scare me. I still don't know who was in the apartment when the gun went off. I'm back to the only truth that I know: trust no one. 'Do you really believe there's anything to incriminate me? There is no proof, no evidence. Nothing.' He sounds like a well-seasoned lawyer and I sense that I'm losing the battle.

'Maybe you're right.' I say, as the food arrives. I can't force a confession. A lion wouldn't give up his catch for another, wouldn't walk towards a female with a carcass in its mouth and drop it down at her feet. I need another line of attack and should have had him followed.

'I must have got my facts wrong,' I say, hoping he'll accept a faux apology.

'People say all sorts of things they don't mean and hear things they shouldn't, or listen to lies.' He looks at me intently. I cut the schnitzel, burying the knife into the breadcrumbs and slicing through the flesh of the veal. The knife slides through to the plate. I bring the piece to my mouth and take a bite. 'So,' he says, 'how are your studies going?'

'It's difficult to juggle everything, but if I work on assignments in the evenings I can keep up. I don't sleep much, anyway.'

'Oh,' he says, almost as a question. I don't respond. 'And what are you working on at the moment?'

I swallow a pulverised piece of meat and purse my lips.

'I'm working on exhibition, museum work and the art trade modules at the moment.'

'Interesting,' he says.

'The art trade lectures are always good and my current assignment is based on art trade and patterns in Europe.' I still feel irritated.

'What are you going to do with all this knowledge when you've finished?'

'I don't know. I took the course because it's a subject I am passionate about. A curator of a museum, perhaps, or a trader. I don't know.' I know I can't legitimately take on anything above board.

'Art belongs, of course, in museums,' he says, almost provocatively.

'I don't agree with you. Museums have no intrinsic right over private individuals, especially if it has been looted.'

'Looted?'

'Yes,' I say. 'Why should a work of art be kept in a museum for the public to enjoy when it could be appreciated by a private collector, an avid art lover? Some of the paintings in galleries in Vienna were looted during the occupation in the nineteen thirties and they belong to the families of those who went through ...'

'The Holocaust,' he says, finishing my sentence.

'Don't you think they should be returned to their rightful owners?'

'That depends,' he says.

'On what, exactly?' I feel myself bristling.

'On when they were taken, and from whom, and whether there are any surviving relatives.' He takes a large bite of steak and drinks his wine.

'What if your grandparents had fled the country? What

if they had been promised their precious belongings once they had crossed the border? Don't you think that if they never saw them again, those paintings should be returned, at least, to you?'

'I think that, by that stage, they belong in the public domain,' he says. 'Liesl, so much time has passed. It's impossible to tell from records which exhibits are stolen and which are legitimate.' His dismissal of it makes me feel a rage I rarely ever experience. I suspect a lot of his nonchalance is a deliberate provocation, a game of cat and mouse.

Chapter 16

The evening light in my apartment stretches out across the wood floor, leaving long shadows. A warm wind moves the curtains momentarily and I feel a sense of peace here in the quiet space, something that I rarely feel around people. I find people endlessly frustrating and unpredictable. I pour a large vodka and watch the clear liquid hit the sides of the glass, slipping between ice cubes. I swill the glass, listening to the ice clink. It's a habit I cannot break. The vodka cools as it mixes with the ice, a contrast to the burn I feel as I take the first swig, my throat numbing as I drain the glass.

I get up and close the window, then slump onto the sofa and boot up the laptop, kicking my feet up towards the window end. I think about the toothbrush on the floor. When I look at simple objects – the door lock, the living room curtain, the window, the bathroom sink – I see misplaced items or the curtain blowing in the breeze, as though someone is still in the apartment. I go over to check that the window is shut and the lock in place, as though my eyes deceive me. My line of vision shifts and moves with the night shadows, a delicate dance of terrifying shapes.

I should use the internet cafe, to avoid detection, but I'm too tired and uneasy about what I now have to do. I log in, using an encrypted password. This will scramble my password so that it's unreadable by hackers. Imagine all that hard work stored on the server. If a hacker gets inside, all your efforts go to waste and your username and password are sold on the open market to the highest bidder. The thought makes me shudder. I have to return the works of art to the rightful owners and time is not on my side. I search for looted art in Austria in 1939.

Hans has sewn seeds of doubt in my mind. I need to check. Just this once, I need to check that I'm not deceived. I always trust my judgement, but his manner has made me waver, made me doubt my own beliefs. I'll go to the cathedral tomorrow and ask for strength of mind, for a resolve that I know I will need. There it is, a page from the search engine on articles of Klimts at the Belvedere, and Schieles at the Leopold. I click on the article which cites the outrage of Herr Leopold. He does, of course, defend his collection and the need for the public to own, and view, these priceless works. He sounds like Hans. Art belongs with its owners, however small and unknown they may be in the art world. It belongs with those who understand its value and I realise I have to move the paintings, not from the museums to the dead drops, but from the museums to their owners.

I log off, close the lid of the laptop and reach for a pack of cigarettes. I take the lighter with the cigarettes to the kitchen and open the window. The night air is still and I feel nothing against my cheeks. There is no movement. I hear the hum of the fridge and the whir of the computer in the other room as the fan kicks in. Crickets start up their high-pitched friction from somewhere outside, beyond the window, and I hear the slow flow of traffic and distant music, thudding from a club in town. I used to go every week. Now, I no longer have the time or the inclination. I feel old, despite still being in my twenties. Something about the stress of the job and juggling shifts keeps me from the party atmosphere that infuses the city each summer and every weekend. It's a life for those who are carefree and with time on their hands.

I run my left thumb across the metal wheel of the lighter and it joins in with the chorus of sounds from the crickets, momentarily, and for long enough to produce a flame. I pull out one Memphis and circle my lips around the end; a familiar manoeuvre, reminding me that I'm home. The alluring scent of smoke, as the end lights up, signals for me to relax, to rest my mind and to focus on inhaling and exhaling, and on nothing but the evening lights and the sound of silence. I'm glad, in these moments, to live alone and not be cramped into a shared apartment with other unwashed students, desperate for the next club scene, in search of a life partner, a soul mate. I need no one but myself, and the sharpness of a mind ready to up sticks and move on, if needed. It's a precarious life, and one I realise that Hans must lead, and for similar reasons. I suspect his employers are more reasonable and reliable, that they don't send him on dangerous missions, just standard insurance fraud and illegal removal of cultural property. These are the words we've been taught in class, but my life is not textbook, more a string of random events that have led me to work for a man who frames his own murder and gives orders that are so removed from his own hand, that he is unreachable. How I came to this underworld is one thing, but now I need to move the art back to its owners, if I want to salvage any thread of buried conscience or human decency.

Chapter 17

I take the number 42 tram out of the city centre from Schottentor towards Antonigasse. Heat fills the carriage and there are no seats. I walk towards the back and stand. I prefer the back because it's easier to get off and walk from Spitalgasse towards the University. The main campus is on the ring in town, but the Art History department is nestled between Spitalgasse, Sensengasse and Alser Strasse, with Ostarrichipark backing onto it from the rear at the southern end. There is a short distance along Universitatstrasse between the two, and the walk past the Votivkirche – which the tourists mistake for Stephansdom, because of its ornate roof tiles – and past the Sigmund Freud Park and the Votivpark.

Once past the entrance, the courtyard opens to a grand display of cream, painted buildings with large brick fronting. The buildings loom high in the skyline. Trees and benches line the paths and bikes lean precariously up against railings. I should buy a bike and save on the cost of travel, but I enjoy the trams with their rattle and hum, the soothing vibrations at the end of the day, the drum of traffic on either side, as we sweep through the city and weave our way through the rush hour traffic. I like watching passengers reading travel guides and novels, speaking to loved ones or staring out into the darkness, decompressing from a day's work.

I clutch my notes and folder, armour for the long lecture ahead. I enjoy studying, but while my mind is full of thoughts of Albert and Hans, and the mystery of Maria's words, I would rather be elsewhere. I need to be alone to think without the distraction of other people's voices. The lock on the door of my apartment, the open window, the shooting in Albert's apartment, the gun, the body, the body on the underground, the assault outside the library, these are all signs, signs that I have to think and move quickly, but there are still tasks I have to fulfil each day – the café, my course, the gallery, Albert. Albert.

His name refuses to budge. I take a seat towards the back of the lecture theatre. As my thoughts turn to Hans, I wonder whether he has lied to me. I want to trust him, I want to believe his words, but I can't help feeling a chill each time I see his face, in the café or outside a shop or gallery, each time I bump into him. Is it calculated? Are there really that many coincidences in life? Omama had a phrase, 'You can't force your own will on the universe.' I agree with her to a point, you can create a world in your mind that is ordered, where things are structured. I can tell myself that he didn't follow me, but my instinct says otherwise. I feel I can't trust him and I'm usually right. What Maria has told me about his possible links to an insurance company sounds contrived. They say dogs return to their own vomit. Am I right in continuing to follow Albert's orders? Did he try to kill me? Did he miss and hit the man I left bleeding out on the apartment floor? I don't know anything for certain.

The lecture is on the movement of art between galleries: the logistics, the cost of museum loans and the specific care needed with different pieces. I listen carefully in the hope that he will tell me something that will help me to move the pieces I'm to lift for Albert while they are on loan. This is the easiest time to move a painting. There's usually less security. We loan out many pieces and they are less likely to be missed if they are out of our hands. Keeping it simple is the key. Professor Zimmerman is slow and steady in his pace. 'The way that each item is displayed,' he says, 'the way that a painting is secured to the wall or in a display case, this must be approved by the Registrar of the lending gallery in advance.' His eyes sparkle and he brushes his beard with his right hand. He describes the way some pictures will be glazed, while others may require a physical barrier to be placed in front of them for protection. There's no protection from a thief, not a good one.

I think of the vaults of the Leopold gallery, and I wonder whether I can move the looted paintings before they're stored in the recesses of the building. Zimmerman explains that the logging must be thorough and precise and has to be checked and rechecked. The Borrower must credit the original owner, or the lending gallery of the painting, in their publications and catalogues. They then need to provide the lending gallery with two copies of the exhibition catalogue as soon as it has been published. This is not part of my job remit, but I listen anyway. It will be useful. I like reading the small print under the painting notes on the wall and I feel a particular joy when I see that it belongs to a 'private collector.' I feel less excited when I read 'Acquired by …'

His circular glasses partially conceal his eyes, small pin pricks of ice blue. He has a kind face and an unsteady walk as he moves across the room. He is talking about the framing, glazing and micro-climates required for different kinds of art. The medium used and the age of the painting makes a difference. 'Various checks,' he says, 'these have to be made in order to accurately assess the security at the premises before a loan is dispatched.' He fails to mention that these include checks on access routes into the exhibition space, although he does cover environmental conditions, like lighting, humidity and temperature. He brushes over the physical security of the building, which is critical, but I'm more aware of this than most. He also doesn't mention the number and type of security staff employed or their training. It's one of the first things I check, always. 'If required improvements to security cannot be made, then a potential loan may be withdrawn,' he says, and I realise that I'm premature. My mind works too quickly with my own experience of the risks they try to teach us. No one fully understands the true extent of these risks.

Other students are scribbling notes while I make the odd mark on my page while staring out of the window across the courtyard. I wonder whether I can do this single-handedly and without trace. With Hans and Albert hot on my tail, it will be difficult, but I can rise to any challenge given the right climate. When the heat is up, I home in on the precise details. The joy of working alone is that no one interferes. Albert has always trusted me.

I return to writing notes on cataloguing and care of canvases and frames. Professor Zimmerman's tone rises, as though talk of the paintings gives him a thrill. He and I have this in common, a love of Art and the world in which it moves. 'Transport,' he says with a degree of gusto, 'this is sometimes outside your hands as a gallery curator. It depends on who has been hired.' Yes, it really does. No one has any idea how much I already know. He spins his pencil, as a magician would spin a wand to make an animal appear from a hat or from behind a screen.

'A Security Advisor will need to inspect the place where a piece is being loaned. This part is vital,' he says, but it's all vital. He loses me at the point where he mentions the *UNESCO Convention on the Means of Prohibiting and Preventing the Illicit Import, Export and Transfer of Ownership of Cultural Property, 1970*. He has no idea what I do. He would be horrified.

I love the fact that I can move in broad daylight in legitimate circles, and look clean. It's a deception that feels like a drug.

Chapter 18

The Leopold is quietest on a Monday. I enter the building for a four hour shift. Light streams in from the skylight and I wonder how it might have felt for Herr Leopold to have opened the gallery in 2001, only years before his death, with five decades of collected works of art from the first half of the 20th century. I wonder what he might have envisaged before it was built: a building with clean lines and an atrium to let the light in, or something grander, perhaps, a castle or a renaissance hallway, something Florentine with a beautiful symmetry of columns, pilasters and lintels, domes and frescos to revive a Golden Age of Sorts; the rebirth of Schiele.

The gallery shows the gradual transformation from the *Wiener Secession*, or *Art Nouveau* movement in Austria to *Expressionism*. Schiele and Kokoschka are some of my favourites. The gallery exhibits many of the major Austrian works of art from the 19th and 20th centuries. It's a treasure trove. Visitors viewing the gallery swirl around me. I pay attention to their movements and colours, whirling dervishes that spin through the display of monochrome prints of life in the seventies by a relatively unknown photographer. The images do not fail to draw crowds and photography seems to draw a certain type of person. They move through the exhibition swiftly and with a critical eye. There's an absence of the lingering admiration I observe when the masters are on display, where the viewer draws in close as though breathing in the scent of the resins and the oils, then steps back with the expectation that the whole picture will become clear from a distance. The larger paintings tend to pull the viewer in one more time as though an invisible coil attached to the body draws it towards the painting and propels it away, only to repeat the movements until the person ceases to move at the point of equilibrium.

I'm familiar with the locations of the cameras, but a quick check reminds me and keeps me focused. I know the times and shifts between guards. By my watch I have four minutes left. I move towards the Kokoschka painting, *Sonnenuntergang*, Sundown. I know the colours and the tones. If I close my eyes, I can see the contrasting colours, the pinks and the orange glow of sundown against the darker blues of the rippling water and the boats along the river. The painting is a flow of movement, the sun flickering between clouds, the skies and water swirling in eddies, refusing to stand still. It's an energetic and engaging piece. I can see why it might have been taken, although how it was labelled *degenerate art* goes far beyond my comprehension. He had to flee Vienna to Prague and then England, because he was labelled a *degenerate* by the Nazis. It's difficult to imagine that Kokoschka's first commissions were postcards and drawings for children, which he drew whilst at Vienna's School of Applied Arts. Ironically, this was the same school that rejected Hitler, as he failed the entry exam. Kokoschka, heavily influenced by artists like Klimt, Schiele and Van Gogh, had his work quickly picked up as he moved on to portraits of the rich and famous within Viennese society. I believe his tempestuous affair with Alma inspired much of his art. Many artists are passionate and impulsive. I don't have the time or the temperament for either.

The guards shift floors every two hours, some moving constantly, others spending five to ten minutes in each room. Security cameras are only located in some of the rooms and not in this one. I scan the room. A guard with a white shirt, red badge and military style grey trousers with a heavy seam up the sides speaks into his headset and moves on. I've timed his movements. He wouldn't look out of place in a prison. I don't recognise him and his uniform is fresh. He must be new.

I pull the painting from the wall and cut it out of the frame in minutes. Surprisingly, it is not alarmed, but I know which ones are. I roll the fabric and slide it under my coat. Unnoticed, and with the camera lens blocked by a dividing wall, I walk briskly towards the exit and out onto the street. It's that easy. Once down the staircase, I unfold the travel bag, which I left tucked away, push the painting into the base and zip it shut. My actions feel crude and I remind myself that the rightful owner is a Martha Neumann, who fled Vienna in 1938, arriving in London. The painting, seized by the Nazis, was later auctioned and picked up for the Leopold. I'm returning this treasure to its rightful owner, now her granddaughter, Maya, and attempting to bring some good from what was an unlawful situation. Perhaps it's a way of easing my conscience. The method of cutting the painting and the risk of damage leaves me cold but I have no other option. I refuse to be compared to thieves who have no care for cultural property or for the heritage or our antiquities. The way that they work is brutal. The Isabella Gardner Museum heist in 1990 involved two men disguised as police officers. They took thirteen works in eighty-one minutes. You can't do the job carefully in that time. I'm pretty sure it's organised crime and that there was a hit list.

It's how we work, although I work alone as much as I can. I don't trust anyone not to mess things up, there's too much at stake. I can only imagine the damage now. They've never been found and it's unlikely they will have been kept flat or in the required fifty percent humidity levels and at twenty-one degrees. The damage, especially to the edges, could now be catastrophic. It's the largest heist yet and worth around 500 million dollars. The irony of the title of one of the paintings stolen, Rembrandt's *Christ in the Storm on the Sea of Galilee*, is not lost on me. The frame left behind, from a workshop in London, had previously been altered with material that had been removed from the inside edges of the frame to accommodate the size of the painting, a chipping away and an alteration of history.

I look up and see an outline of a figure, the same outline that I saw when I went into the library, the outline that moved closer, tackled me, then fled. I turn, hide behind the steps, and wait. A few minutes pass and I disappear through the crowds outside Museumsquartier bar towards the Volkstheater underground instead of the planned route to the closer station of Museumsquartier. I pass tourists sipping espressos and rotating maps, heads tilted sideways and sun worshippers, sprawled on awkward shaped purple blocks scattered across the central courtyard. They notice neither me or my bag with its hidden masterpiece. The purple blocks are gathered up and turned into an ice bar in the winter months, selling vodka shots in ice glasses. The beat of the bass from over-sized speakers makes your glass shake in the bitter cold of January.

I turn, occasionally, to see if I'm being followed, but I appear to have lost the figure. I take a right turn under the arches along Berggasse and swing right again under the purple U2 sign and sprint down the escalators to Volkstheater station, almost knocking over tourists and a group of schoolchildren. I manage to jump on the underground carriage as the train doors close. I can feel the blood in my veins, hot and furious. I slump into a corner seat, clutching the bag, and look out of the window into a wall of darkness. I can see only my own reflection and a few others, but mainly the red seats, the silver metal of the poles and the darkness of the tunnel walls.

A figure is sitting further back in the carriage and, for a moment, he seems recognisable and familiar. I look quickly, and without turning my head, only looking through the reflection of the glass, and I see Hans. He is reading a book. My stomach scrunches. I feel a sense of doom. It's usual to bump into people you know in Vienna on occasion, but the number of times I've seen him is not a coincidence. I want to turn, to drop the bag, walk towards him and challenge him, but I can't. I almost missed this train myself. Did he get on ahead of me? I wonder whether he might have been the figure who attacked me outside the library or whether he's been inside my apartment, uninvited. My mind is cast back to my lunch with Hans and his interest in art. I consider the idea that he too may be a thief, but it's more likely that he is following me under contract, and this thought becomes more real. It's difficult to react normally around him.

I have to pass this Schiele on to Neumann's granddaughter. I have memorised her address in case it's not safe to write down her location. I don't keep any record of current contacts, locations or paintings. I have to work carefully, quickly and without leaving any trail. I have to work as though I no longer exist.

The train is approaching Karlsplatz which is the end of

119

the line. I glance towards the figure and am certain it's Hans. The train lurches to a halt. I dig into my pocket for a tissue and wait for the figure to get up and leave. He steps on to the platform and moves towards the steps. I wait a few more seconds then follow, clutching the bag. I can no longer see him on the platform. I reach the bottom step. The sunlight streaming down is almost blinding. I look up and see him at the top. He turns right and vanishes. I pick up speed, running two or three steps at a time to the exit, and realise that I can't follow him, not with the painting on me. Turning sharply to the left, I walk towards the apartment. I know that I'm not safe.

Chapter 19

The apartment building is empty during the day so that my footsteps echo against the spiral stone staircase and sounds ricochet off the walls. I reach my door and turn the key in the lock. It revolves, twice, always twice, except for the one occasion when it only turned by one revolution and stopped. I feel haunted by that one occurrence each time I enter.

I draw a breath and kick the door back. The bread and milk from breakfast have been left out on the side. I must have remembered to put the ham and cheese slices back in the fridge. Half a tomato spews seeds onto the draining board in a limp explosion, but it has kept its form, the skin still plush and sun-drenched red. The coffee filter is switched off. It was the last thing I remember doing as I left. The glass pot sits comfortably on its heating ring with half a pot of cold, resin-coloured fluid, a sludgy ring slightly higher up, evidence of its original level at seven o'clock this morning before I drained half the contents in three instalments into my favourite black and white striped mug. I prefer monochrome, not so much in art, but in life. It makes a statement. There's a boldness in the way that it cancels out colour.

I hear footsteps in the stairway and move slowly towards the wide-angle spy hole in the door. With one eye pressed against it, I see my eyelashes blinking back at me, followed by the junk mail delivery boy. I drop my shoulders and exhale until my lungs are empty. I go back into the kitchen, fill the kettle and flip the switch. I've forgotten to kick my shoes off and, instead of lining them up neatly, I fling them under the bench with the row of house shoes and a box of tools. A knock at the door makes me lurch forward. I could pretend to be out, but I look again through the spy hole and see the postman with a package. I turn the lock and swing the door back. He smiles, gives me a small brown package and thrusts a machine at me, signalling for me to scribble my name on the screen.

I write a scrawl, which is as much as I can manage with a plastic stick. The words don't line up with where the tip touches the screen.

'Danke sehr,' I say.

He nods, 'Schönen Tag.'

His words bring me comfort. I swing the door shut, its length stretching from the wood floor to a few feet below the high ceiling. These old Viennese buildings bring a grandeur into the fabric of the city, a signature of an era which no longer exists. Thick walls keep rooms warm in the winter and retain a blissful cool in the hot summer months. On the days when the city reaches forty degrees I rarely leave the building, preferring instead to spend the day curled over my laptop with a pot of coffee, wearing nothing by a flimsy vest top and knickers, occasionally rinsing my feet in the shower to cool off and splashing my face with cold water. I run the tap and hold the pulse points of my wrists under the flow, my body heat rinsed away, draining into underground pipes.

I place the parcel on the side, make a coffee, resisting the urge for a vodka, and take the bag into the living room. I unzip it, carefully. My hands feel clammy and my breathing shallow. I feel a tingle of excitement as the colour of the canvas stretches out in front of me. The sense of danger, and the knowledge that I'll return the painting to its rightful owner, is unmatched. Then I remember Albert. I wonder whether to move and stay with someone outside the city, retreat to a safe location. But I can't leave, not yet.

I take the canvas out of the bag, place it onto the rug and gently roll it out. It's simply breathtaking, the colours with their dark tones, captivating. Although it goes against everything I've learned, I touch the painting, stroking the edges then its surface, I feel the undulations left behind in the oils, moulded by a pallet knife, the artist's weapon.

My mind turns to the Kokoschka and to Martha Neumann's granddaughter, Maya, and to the gallery. They will have noticed the gap on the wall by now, found the empty frame on the floor, and imagined it to be an act of savagery performed by a guard. I should feel guilt but I don't. I fix my eyes on the desk, pull out a stool and pick up a pen, an envelope and a pad of thick white sheets of paper. Taking a ballpoint pen, I start to write her address on an envelope:

Maya Neumann
Derry Court
386 Streatham High Road
London
SW16 6AU
United Kingdom

I tear off a sheet of paper and place my right hand down on the page, as though preventing it from straying, the fingers of my left hand gripping the pen. I could have found her email address or called her, but I avoid leaving a trail and I will ask her to destroy this letter once she has read the contents. Similarly, I will tear up and burn any response from her. I could not write until I had the painting in my hands. I found her address a month ago. I had gone to a deteriorating internet café and paid a euro for the privilege of using a small, dirty computer, touched by sticky fingers, boxed into a tiny section of a café. Livestock forced into small spaces might feel the same sense of panic. While I was there, the place was empty and I kept my gloves on. I found her address after a short search. Thoughts of her grandmother fleeing this country reminded me that I was doing the right thing. Nothing should force a citizen out of their land. Nothing.

My pen hovers over the page and I wonder what will convince her, after this length of time, that a complete stranger is offering their family's lost painting. I am a messenger. I've been transformed, at the very least, from an art thief. I have to believe this is a restoration of sorts.

Dear Maya,

Forgive my lack of manners in contacting you without introduction. I have learned of your grandmother, Martha, her need to flee Austria as well as the loss of her treasured family art. I have in my possession a work by Kokoschka, Sonnenuntergang, originally hers. Now, by way of your family connections, it is yours. It's an exquisite work.

Kind regards,

Liesl Baumgartner

I hesitate for a moment and return the pen to its holder. Maya has to believe that I have the work before she will respond.

Chapter 20

Hans has asked to see me. I suspect it has something to do with the painting. I know he's following me but I can't trace him back to a specific employer. I reach Café Schwarzenburg and push through the doors, grateful to step out of the rain. The cafe is older and darker than Heiner, a step back in time with its marbled walls, sweeping arches and windows that stretch up to a glittering, tiled ceiling with glass chandeliers – weeping willows of ice droplets, catching the light.

A lady in a mustard yellow sweater and half-moon glasses reads a paper taken from a wooden rack, the pole still running down through the centre. Her demeanour is gruff and undistracted as the waiter arrives with a steaming cup of coffee and a large butter croissant. She fails to acknowledge him, or the coffee, eyes fixed to the pages of *Wiener Zeitung*. The word 'Schwarzenburg' frames her head across the mirror behind, arching across from one window to another. She notices neither myself or the dog belonging to another customer. The dog ferrets around beneath the table.

The waiter slips away towards the kitchen carrying a silver tray, his moustache, dark and curled at the edges, a facial topiary of sorts. I look out of the window at the station-like cubed clock on Kärntner Ring with its four faces, high on a post, lamplights splayed out from the top. It's half past ten and I am on time. I'm never late. Lateness makes me uncomfortable. I was once delayed on the U-bahn, when we were stuck in a tunnel between stations, and was gripped by claustrophobia. Hans arrives shortly after me, wearing a shirt, hair slicked back. He usually wears jeans and a t-shirt outside his Heiner uniform. I hope he hasn't dressed up for my sake. I smile as he looks across toward me. He heads to the coat rack and hangs up his jacket and umbrella, then joins me at the table. He pulls out a chair and squeezes into the seat. The table arrangements are confining. A long line of tables dominates the centre of the café and leaves only narrow passages to reach the edges of the room.

'You weren't at the café last week,' he says, as though it's a question.

'How have you been?' I ask.

'Where were you?'

'I didn't feel well. I took some time off. I'm fine.'

'Oh,' he says, his curiosity irritating.

'How is everyone?'

'Thanks. They're fine. They miss you. The customers were asking after you. You look good.'

'I didn't think the customers would notice my absence.'

'They do. The gentleman who buys the pies ...'

'Markus.'

'Yes. He was asking for you.'

'I'm sure everything is running smoothly. I'll be back next week, no doubt packaging tortes and taking orders of Gugelhupf.'

He raises his eyebrows and looks at the waiter. 'An espresso for me and ...' He stretches out a hand in my direction.

'I'll have one, too,' I say. 'Hans, what were you doing in England?'

'Working for an insurance company,' he says, eyebrows raised.

'And Graz?'

'Economics. I've already told you.' I know they have a centre for private investigations but I can't push him. Not yet. 'Why?' he asks.

'I was just curious. You seem out of place working in the café.'

'So do you,' he says, without hesitation. 'It pays the rent. You?'

'You know I'm juggling studies with the gallery, but they don't have enough hours. The job at Heiner is a top up. Given the choice, though, I'd still do both. I like the gallery, but the bustle of the café and the scent of coffee, it's a buzz.'

'Really?'

'Hans, my life is pretty uneventful. I don't have family or friends and I spend most of my time alone. I don't go out, and I like the noise and banter of the café.' Hans smiles. There's a flicker of light in his eyes, a look that's been absent for a while. 'The truth is, I like my life the way it is and I don't need company. I like to be alone.' It has always been safer to work alone. Solitude is safety, in the same way that the dark was a form of safety for my parents when the Gestapo took control of Vienna. Omama always told me that they felt safer after dark. When the lights were out, it was easier to hide.

'Where would we be without the cafe?' he says, 'On a Pacific Island, perhaps, or working in a law firm somewhere more pacy, more cosmopolitan. New York? Berlin? I don't know.'

'I won't leave this city,' I say. 'It's part of the fabric of who I am.' I need to hear the sound of the trams, watch the flow of the Danube on its journey towards the Black Sea. Black as asphalt.'

'Interesting,' he says. 'I don't see you as a person who would feel attached or rooted anywhere.'

'We rarely really know people, Hans. We like to think we do, but we don't, not really.' Everybody hides a part of themselves from others.

'You surprise me.' He half smiles, his eyes fixed on mine. 'It doesn't sound like any way to live.'

'I know,' I say, feeling the heat in my cheeks. My questions were meant to unearth details about his time in England but I feel as though I'm speaking to a well-seasoned lawyer or worse, a politician.

'Hans, why were you at the café that day, the one behind the church on Graben?'

'I told you,' his voice hardens, 'I happened to be passing and saw you through the window. Your face looked ...'

'What?' I feel myself bristle.

'I don't know. You looked lost. I wanted to come in and sit with you.'

'Why do I keep seeing you outside work? I know Vienna isn't a big city, but you don't bump into the same person that often.'

'Maybe you're being a little paranoid.'

'Just aware of my surroundings.'

'I don't have any other answer,' he says, lips pursed, eyes squeezed almost shut. 'And not one that would satisfy you.'

It's beginning to feel like a bad first date. I phase out of what he's saying and order a slice of rich, dark chocolate torte to have with the espresso. I don't usually have a taste for sugar, but this morning it's exactly what I need. A combination of late nights, stress and trying to track down Maya has left me feeling listless. I don't know if Hans has noticed. My eyes are circled with the grey of too many early hours and late nights, too much coffee and not enough food. I lose my appetite when I'm under pressure.

Hans leans back as I order, as though settling himself in for the rest of the day. He has a self-assurance that makes me uncomfortable. I might look this way to the outside world, but most of us rarely ever are, not at the core. My job is unnerving and I've grown used to hiding much of my life. Much of myself.

I no longer know where a truth ends and an untruth begins which is partly how I manage the disjointed parts of my life, like concealing a disease from relatives. When a painting doesn't fit together to produce a complete work, the viewer fills in the gaps, usually in the way that the artist intends. It's almost certainly the reason the Ancient Greeks created the optical illusion and built their temples with slanting roofs and bulging pillars. Dutch artist, Samuel van Hoogstraten, in his perspective box in London's National Gallery, shows the painted world through a small hole. People paint what they want us to see. Austrian art historian, Gombrich, asks why varying ages and nations represent art so differently. We only see certain truths, missing untruths. Vermeer used a dead-colour technique, a distribution of dark and light before he applied colour. Light and dark underlies everything in life, a spread of good and evil across a canvas. We create illusions of life: Light. Dark.

'What were you doing in the Leopold,' he asks.

I almost spit out my coffee. 'The Leopold?' I say, to stall the conversation.

'Yes. Yesterday. I saw you leaving.'

'I had to drop in to check the rota and pick up a coat I'd left behind,' I say, trying not to let my breathing or expression change.

'I didn't see you leave with a coat.'

'It was in my bag. What is this? I'm not sure why you're interrogating me.'

'You said you were ill. I was just curious.' He's too curious and now he's becoming annoying. I fail to understand how he charms the girls at work, or the customers. I wipe away crumbs of chocolate from my lips. 'Here,' he says, grabbing the napkin from my hand and wiping my mouth gently. It feels oddly comforting, but I pull back and fold my arms.

'So, what are you seeing next?' I ask.

'You mean exhibitions?'

'Yes, you said you liked art.' I wonder whether he needs the reminder.

'I'm heading to the History of Art Museum.'

'What are you going to see?'

'There's an exhibition by the artist, Glenn Brown.'

'Glenn Brown?' I feel annoyed that he's throwing an artist, unknown to me, into the conversation. This is deliberate.

'He's a British artist. He paints work inspired by science fiction and history.' His tone is becoming professorial. It makes me agitated. He might be bright, but I'm smarter.

'What kind of work? What's his style?'

Hans smiles, as though he's won a battle. 'Figures, mostly, and sculptures. They are painted with thick impasto and thin, swirling brushstrokes to create an illusion of flat, almost photographic, images. His work unsettles, like his painting, *Nausea*.

I could respond with something he does not know, but it's not worth it. Instead, I nod, drain my coffee and get up to leave.

'So soon?' he says.

'See you next week,' I say, without looking at him, and I work my way through the tables to the door.

Chapter 21

This morning Albert's instructions lead me to Herr Schneider. Given the previous revelation about his brother, I decide to slip a penknife into my pocket. It's a large Swiss army knife with a deep green sheen and the initials H.C. etched into it along one side in a gold italic font: Herbert Christoph, my father's Christian names. Although it's not an ideal weapon, I'm uncomfortable carrying a gun into a situation like this. If you're going to have a weapon turned on you, a knife is a better defence than a gun. You can reach a running target with a gun, but a knife requires the victim to stand close. In this line of work, these are the details you need to keep in mind. Think ahead, observe, predict. Never neglect the details.

The curtains are open as I reach the gate. The tram begins to travel uphill towards Grinzing where grapes are crushed in the vineyards to make Sturm at this time of year. Sturm is a dangerous drink. A product of the early stages of wine production, its rapid fermentation means that it must be consumed within a few days, otherwise the bottle will explode. The street is strangely silent this morning with an absence of voices, cars and movement. I wonder if it's because of the storm clouds, then I remember that it's a public holiday. The door opens as I walk through the gate and up the path. His face appears ragged and pained.

'Guten Morgen,' he says.

'Gruss Gott.'

He nods and opens the door wide, stretches out an arm and sweeps it back into the hallway, a pendulum rocking back and away from equilibrium, a gesture which I assume is designed to beckon me inside.

I put one foot in the door and wait. Again, he swings his arm backwards and, with it, goes my second foot, an invisible force pulling me into the house. He turns away without looking at me and walks off down the hallway. I follow him into his sitting room and position myself, as before, in the armchair opposite. I look again at the pictures on the wall and wait for him to speak. An uncomfortable silence fills the air while he repositions his bifocals and picks up a book from the reading table beside him. His hair catches the light, silver threads with a sheen, possibly from some kind of wax or cream. Mine is left to hang loose around my neck. I don't add any products and I don't like the sticky texture of gels. I get ready in under ten minutes, doing away with all extravagances, though the curls make brushing a bit of a chore. I prefer people to look natural, unpainted. My lashes don't need coatings of thick mascara and I like my hair to look ruffled.

I notice the kink in his hair, exactly like the hair on the head of the body at the station. Does he think I killed his brother? Does he know that I took the priceless piece of jewellery? The star brooch was valued at around eighteen thousand euros when I sent it, anonymously, to the Dorotheum auction house. The stones were diamonds, as I had thought. Whether or not they had once belonged to Empress Elisabeth is impossible to discern, but their value was no surprise.

Herr Schneider looks directly at me while I hold my breath. He doesn't speak and I stare back at him.

'Liesl,' he says, 'did you know him?'

'Who?'

'My brother.' He waits for a hint of recognition. 'The body at the station?'

'No, it was a job. Albert sent me to retrieve a note from him.'

'It wasn't Albert who sent you though, was it?'

'I don't know what you mean.' I remember the body in the apartment, the attack outside the national library, the sightings of Hans, and I have no idea who set me up. Who would have sent me to Stephansplatz, if not Albert?

Herr Schneider looks at me and I feel cold. I put my right hand into the back pocket of my trousers and wait.

'Liesl, what makes you sure that it was Albert who sent you to me?'

'The note was from him. You read it.'

'It was signed from him but have you ever met him? Have you seen him sign his name?'

'Herr Schneider, I'm not sure that you can make that kind of judgement.'

'I see,' he says, and stands up and walks over to the window behind me.

I turn, an instinctive move. I remember walking towards the painting in the apartment and hearing the gunshot. What if it was Herr Schneider who set up the meeting and not Albert? I run through my first meeting with him: the note I found on his brother, the request to plant the note in a potted narcissi, the secrecy. Why would he set up his own meeting and, if it was not Albert, who sent me? If Albert doesn't exist, am I working for Herr Schneider? What about Maria? And Hans? If they're involved, how?

'Coffee?' he asks, nonchalantly, as though trying to put

me at ease, but nothing will make me relax, not now. I need to get out of here.

'No. Thank you. I don't have time, not today.'

'Yes you do,' he says, to my surprise, and he strides off in the direction of the kitchen. I want to run, but I need more information from him before I leave.

'All right, but it will have to be quick.' He is gone before I can finish.

'Yes. Yes,' he says, waving an arm, his voice disappearing down the corridor.

The ticking clock on the mantelpiece is all I can hear, and the pulsing of blood inside my skull. I think of the body at the station – Herr Schneider's brother, contorted, lifeless – and the body in the apartment, Albert's apartment, although I don't really know. Is Albert my boss, or has he been constructed by Herr Schneider, or someone else, to mislead me and wipe all traces of any operation?

I think of Maria's information about the Jewish art plundered during the Anschluss. I must stay focused. I have to return the painting to the family in London. I can't let this man, or thoughts of Hans, throw me off course. I know my work isn't exactly legitimate, but the realisation that I've been moving plundered art puts a different spin on things. My conscience won't let me ignore this. Not with all I now know.

'I only have brown sugar,' he says, returning.

'Thank you.' I nod and pull out the small coffee table by my chair. There's a menacing glint in his eyes and I worry about his next move. I decide not to touch the coffee.

'Liesl, you're treading a fine line here. You don't know who you're dealing with, or how dangerous some of these operations are if they go wrong.' He pauses and lowers his glasses, looks over the tops of the rims. 'You wouldn't want to get caught and be taken out of the game, would you?'

'Are you threatening me, Herr Schneider?'

'I'm making you aware of the situation you now find yourself in, and I would warn you to be very careful about any extra-curricular activities, if you understand me. My brother should have been alive when you reached him.'

'But he wasn't and we have to work with what we know. These jobs won't get done unless there is someone to lift the work and deposit it in the dead drops, someone who is prepared to take risks.' We both know I didn't kill him.

'I see. Well, we won't waste any more time. Here,' he says, passing me another note.

'Thank you,' I say, getting up to leave, my coffee cup still full. He grabs my arm.

'We have an understanding now, don't we?' I know that this is anything but a question. I nod and leave swiftly. Out in the light, I open the note from Herr Schneider and read it on the tram to the city centre.

Your life is still in danger. Watch your back. I need the Klimt from the Belvedere. Drop it in the map section. You'll find a way.

The letter is unsigned and it's not Albert's style. I reach my apartment block and jump off the tram. When I insert the key in the box at the bottom of the staircase, it feels stiff. I find a letter stamped with a postmark from London. I climb the stairs, enter the apartment and turn the coffee machine on. I scan the rooms before sitting on the indented end of the sofa. I open the letter, but the handwriting is difficult to decipher.

Dear Liesl,

Thank you for your letter. We had given up hope of ever seeing the painting again. It is hard to believe after so much time has passed but I want to believe you. I will be coming to Vienna in two weeks to visit a niece. I can meet you then if you'll kindly give me a time and a location. I am so very grateful to you. I feel, somehow, that a part of our past has been re-covered.

Maya

I close the letter and fold it back into the envelope. Her words are an uncomfortable reminder that I've been sending art into the wrong hands. I need to work swiftly to return as many stolen works as possible into the hands of their rightful owners. I put the letter down and go into the kitchen, turning off the lights, except a sidelight. I light a single candle on the coffee table. The low light hides parts of the apartment that look sad in daylight: the frayed edges of the sofa, the flaking polish on the wood table, lighter tones of carpet, where I recently moved a bookcase out of the room. I remember Maria telling me about her parents, and I think of mine, only for a moment.

In the kitchen I ignore the pot of coffee, the steam seeping through the top of the machine. I pull a pack of Memphises from a drawer, remove the first in the pack, flip the lighter and hold it between my lips, drawing until the tip is lit. I find an almost drained vodka bottle on the shelf above the sink and pour what's left into a glass tumbler. I take both with me into the living room, kicking off my house shoes on the way through the hall. They land on top of the outdoor shoes and I can't resist going back to put them straight. The candlelight flickers across the walls of the living room. Street lights throw a strip of yellow across the room in a diagonal line. I pull off my sweater, take the soft scarf from the arm of the sofa and wrap it around my neck.

I inhale deeply, allowing the drug to relax my body, then I take a long swig of vodka. The silence – apart from a slow, steady stream of cars and the occasional bus – is what I enjoy most about the late hours of the evening, this and the lack of demands. I savour this time to think over the day's work and plan the next move.

The telephone rings. I want to avoid answering, but find myself instead walking towards the receiver in the hallway. I pick it up, but there is no one on the other end. I put the receiver down, remembering the last empty call, just after the apartment was disturbed. Hans? Albert? Schneider? I don't know.

I switch on the computer. A chill runs down my spine, as though somebody has just passed me, and I turn around. The room is undisturbed: an empty glass, a smouldering Memphis stub in the ashtray, the letter. The light illuminating the floorboards suggests a barricade. I take in a long slow breath and turn back to the computer. I hear the front door rattle and I get up, walk slowly to the latch and peer through the keyhole. There is no one on the other side. I remember Herr Schneider's threats, and the letter telling me to go to Melk, and I wonder if I was unwise to stay.

I sit back down, taking the cigarette stub with me, the tip reminding me of Hans' finger nails, snarled and short. I hear the front door of the main building slam shut, followed by footsteps outside the building. I move over to the window, undo the latch and lean out, but there is no-one on the street. I stand there for a moment, then go back to the computer, leaving the window open, as though I might hear a sound, something, anything that might give me a clue as to who might be tracking my movements. The phone rings every day, about ten to fifteen minutes after I arrive home, as though the caller wants me to know that I have been located.

I pull up the search that tells me that Hitler amassed seven thousand works of art. I suspect this is an underestimation. I read about the locations where many works were stored: in castles, large houses, vaults. The Altaussee salt mines come up in the search. So, too, does the Monastery in Mauerbach and I think about the soiling of the purity of prayer, and the storing of stolen art. I think of what the monks would do if they had found the art, and consider how God may, or may not, cast judgement. The European Art Museum in Linz was a dream never realised. Hitler, I read, aimed to create the largest collection of art, a status symbol to make up for something lacking in his own self-esteem. Frustrated and angry, and rejected by the Art Academy twice, he became a collector of treasures. A child hoarding his toys.

It dawns on me that I've been feeding works to another senseless, power-hungry man which makes it all the more important that I track down the owners of the looted art. It's too late to do anything about the paintings I've already shifted but I can restore some and bring restitution to the families who have suffered.

Chapter 22

I'm hesitant about leaving the building with the painting. Maya will be at the Opera House waiting for me but someone will be close on my tail. I drain the coffee cup and tie my hair up in a knot, then grab a straw sunhat and pull it down over my ears.

I pick up my sunglasses and take one last look at the painting. It is beautiful. There is a busy serenity about the scene – the colours, the texture – that makes me want to linger over it. The buildings on the river banks remind me of a matchbox village I once made. I wonder who might have lived in those by the water with the low orange glow from the sky in the late evening light. And I wonder about the daily rituals of the people. I notice the boats in amongst the blue brushstrokes. Would locals have fished or gossiped about local life there? The river flows through the painting, catching the light as it ripples against the sides of the banks. I wrap the canvas in paper, then in a blanket and lower it carefully into my bag. I pull the zip across reluctantly, my finger lingering before I pull the strap up over my shoulder.

I draw in a deep breath and slide on my sunglasses. I leave the apartment, pulling the door hard behind me. I turn the key twice. I count the turns now. The memory of it being unlocked and relocked makes me check that I've locked it properly. I'm careful to lock and check everything, always. I have to be precise, to not miss a thing, but I slip up on occasion. We all do. Tiredness, distraction, things that pull us away from our focus can all threaten to derail our plans. I remember the toothbrush on the floor, the painting at Albert's. It wasn't his apartment. I see Cezanne's skull and feel cold. I turn the key back the other way to check that it turns twice and lock it again. I resist checking a third time then carry the bag down the stairs, clutching the smaller looped handles. I don't want to risk it sliding off my shoulder. I'm unusually nervous. A dead drop or a painting pick-up from a gallery doesn't usually unsettle me, but I know the history of this painting. The wrong that the Neumanns have suffered makes this transfer absolutely critical. The fate of some of the looted art rests on my shoulders. I feel responsible, a trait I learned from Omama. Anxiety fuels the nights, and I numb it with vodka, cigarettes and coffee. In daylight hours, I can look out over the city and tell myself that what I am doing is legitimate. But it isn't really, it's theft of the worst kind. Cultural theft is a big issue that no one knows how to tackle because there aren't enough experts.

I take a deep breath as I exit the building. I decide against taking the tram and walk into the city towards the Opera House. Heat invades the streets, even this early. The sun pierces through gaps in the high buildings, casting shafts of light across the street. I hear the distant rumble of traffic but our street is quiet at this time of day.

I wonder about the open window and whether someone actually climbed down from the second floor to street level. I try to remember whether I left the latch undone. It may have blown open in the wind. It reminds me of my climb down from the Dorotheum auction house. The Canaletto fake will have been spotted by now. I feel a twinge of guilt about the original, not knowing where it's now located.

It's an odd feeling, giving a stolen painting back to its original owner. Does it make me traitorous or self-righteous? I don't know, but I know that I should feel neither. If I'm a traitor, it's only to Albert. I should remember my job and the countless paintings I've shifted which are probably now in the wrong hands.

I reach the ring and wait at the lights. Delivery lorries and fast cars pass in a steady stream. A couple of boys in a sports car preen themselves, music thudding, drifting out, their eyes concealed, like mine, behind sunglasses. The lights change, I look both ways and cross with tourists and an elderly lady with a trolley. I want to help her but instead I clutch the bag and walk towards the arches above the entrance. My eyes are fixed on people standing on the other side of the road.

At the Opera House a woman with a scarf knotted under her chin stands under one of the arches. She has a neat frame and charcoal coloured hair. Her eyes flicker from side to side, scanning the street. They stop and rest on my bag. I keep walking. She looks up at me. We both half smile and I walk up the few steps to the entrance. We shake hands. She looks at me in disbelief.

'Thank you,' she says, clutching my hand in hers. She holds it then releases her grip. There's sadness in her eyes, a longing.

'My pleasure,' I say, but I feel loss more than relief. Maybe it's her loss I sense. I think about the burnt oranges of the evening light in the painting and I see the orange flicker of the flames that burned so many of the other paintings. I imagine the soldiers mocking, chanting. Her grandmother had so much ripped from her life. I feel my stomach twist. A dove lands in front of us before taking off again into the sky.

'Shall we go to a park? It might be more private,' I say.

She nods, I suspect unable to form any words. I lead us back across the road to Stadtpark. The only people in the park are young children and distracted mothers. They fail to notice our appearance, but I walk around to a quieter area to be safe.

'Thank you,' she says again, her eyes glistening. 'I didn't think I'd ever see it again. My grandmother told me quite a bit about what happened, and she always described the painting. It was one of her strongest childhood memories. It hung in the living room of their family home where it stayed until ...' She didn't need to finish the sentence. 'Can I pay you?' she asks, her eyebrows raised, her pupils narrowing against the sun.

'No. Please. It's yours. I'm only returning it.' I stop myself from saying any more. She knows enough to understand I had access to the painting but she doesn't need more details.

'Thank you. I'm truly grateful.' Her eyes fill with tears. She blinks and reaches towards the bag. 'May I?'

'Yes, of course.' I unzip the bag to reveal the painting but leave it inside. Then I take the strap off my shoulder and hand her the bag. She takes another look and closes the zip. I hold out a hand and she reaches to shake it.

She nods then leans in to hug me. She holds me as though I might be her mother or grandmother, then releases her arms, blinks again, pulls the strap up over her shoulder and turns to walk out of the park. I walk slowly behind her, hanging back until she is gone. I feel a sense of loss, and this time it's not her loss but mine, the loss of my parents and then of Omama. Losing my parents was never explained to me. In my memory they are ghosts of a past I don't remember. My grandmother was my childhood and all that was good about it. Opa, my grandfather, is the reason I studied Art.

Chapter 23

Free of a café shift today, I wander back towards the Opera House, and on to the Albertina gallery. The steps are filled with brightly coloured posters showcasing a cubist exhibition. I take the escalator, gripping the moving handrail and look up towards the gallery entrance. I see Hans and begin to walk, breaking into a run as I reach the top. I can see the back of his head as I push through the crowds. I reach him and pull his arm, but he is not alone. He turns and looks at me, but it is not him. A girl, obscured by the crowds, grabs his arm and scowls at me.

'What's wrong with you?' she shouts.

'I'm sorry. I thought you were a friend.' He is more gracious and tells me not to worry. She is still scowling, pulling him away as though I might be some wild animal. 'I'm sorry,' I say, this time to the girl, but they have already turned away.

I slump down on the steps outside Do and Co, to the side of the entrance. A waiter asks if I need help and I lift a hand to let him know I'm fine. How much else have I mistaken? How many other situations have I misjudged or misremembered? I feel an unfamiliar pain in my chest and clutch my ribs. The waiter brings me a glass of cold water. I wave again. Words fail me. I feel weak, something I rarely feel. He is gone. A cool and welcome breeze picks up, brushing across my skin. Sweat drips from my chin. The heat is intense and my head feels foggy.

I get up, leaving the glass on the table, and nod as the waiter collects it. He disappears back inside and I walk around to the front entrance. It's in the shade. I slip off my shoes and press my feet flat against the cool, hard ground. A small girl coming up the steps stares at my feet and then up at me. She smiles, takes off her shoes and stands next to me but her mother quickly scoops her up like a bird, taking the shoes with her, and carries the girl inside. She looks back at me and smiles. It's an awkward smile, one that tells me she is either uncomfortable with her daughter being near me or embarrassed that she has pulled her away.

I wait, then slip my shoes back on. The queue is short. I buy an inclusive ticket, hoping to see the state rooms. I should have already viewed them. A girl checks my ticket and nods. I feel like an imposter when I'm just visiting a gallery, as though I might be found out, something I don't experience when I'm removing a painting. The Albertina has a peace and a grandeur that's missing from the Leopold. I like to move slowly from one exhibition to the next, drifting and thinking about the paintings, photographs or sculptures. Red carpet stretches ahead and up the stairs between the marble pillars; a yellow brick road of sorts, although I feel more like the tin man than Dorothy.

I reach Duerer's watercolour, The Young Hare, a personal favourite, and stop to look at the form, the curves of its body, the muted colours of the paint and the expression in its eyes. Is it a resignation or a restfulness? The way its ears and fur catch the light has held me captive from a very early age. I linger, taking in the tones and the detail. Each time I look, I notice something new. This time I see flecks of white on its haunches notice the downward curve of its whiskers. I want to stretch out my hand and touch it. It looks at me and away at the same time. I nod, out of deference to the artist, and move on towards the state rooms.

The Hall of Muses opens out into an expanse of dazzling chandeliers and marble statues, ushering me in. Having studied the artist Joseph Kliebe, I know that the statues are sandstone with a mock marble finish. Stucco marble panels and large mirrors adorn the walls, behind statues of Apollo and the Nine Muses. I imagine people dancing and others standing to the sides of the room, talking in hushed tones, tall in elegant dresses. Greek architecture, although grand, feels out of place amongst a Hapsburg collection.

Leaving the Hall, I reach the Study Cabinet of Archduke Ferdinand. The desk is positioned almost in the centre of the room. Immediately, I can see my grandfather writing a letter, head down, eyebrows furrowed, busying himself in 'administrative tasks,' as he called them in a tone of disgust, as though it distracted him from his painting. I see him in his art studio, smell the scent of turpentine from the cloths and the oils, his pallet and knife slathered with paints, waiting to be applied to the next piece of canvas stretched across the frame, his eyebrows straighter now and his eyes alight.

'So, we begin,' he would say, his arm stretched out with a brush, as though he might begin a dance. Oma would call from another room, would he like coffee or something to eat? He'd say no. 'It breaks my concentration. I never paint on a full stomach. Focus on one thing at a time.' And he was right. It's a rule I apply to my own life. I think about the uninterrupted hit of nicotine and alcohol late at night.

Someone is following me. I turn but the room is empty. An eerie silence fills the hall, not a visitor in sight. I feel the presence of generations of emperors and empresses and wonder whether they might have had moments of boredom, days of endless wandering, waiting, socialising. It would have killed me. Empress Sisi loathed court life. My life isn't laid out for me, no agenda dictated by the expectations and etiquette of Viennese high society, only letters with unpredictable next steps.

The image of Opa fades, replaced by the gold-embossed fabric lining of the walls and the bust of a figure deep in thought. I continue on through the rooms until I reach the exit. I decide against going into the cubist exhibition. My mind is preoccupied with the painting, Maya, and how I can gather more works and find their owners. Maria's words of the plunder remain with me. I imagine flames engulfing canvases, see Picasso's faces snarling and twisting until they disappear. *Degenerative Art*, Hitler called it, maybe out of jealousy or a kind or madness. I think of the valuable works of art, layer upon, layer, crammed into monasteries and caves, left festering, unobserved.

I swing the main door open and throw my head up towards the sky. I need to get back to the apartment and find more information on the looted art, then locate the pieces and search for the owners. It won't happen overnight, but moving them one by one, I can make a difference.

Chapter 24

Café Heiner is unusually quiet this morning and Hans hasn't yet arrived. I only notice because I feel more relaxed when he's not around. It's nothing specific, just a sense of unease when he passes or stops to talk. I know he has a shift today. I look at the roster when I arrive. My hours are fixed, but his fluctuate. I don't appreciate many things being fixed, but there's enough uncertainty and spontaneity in the rest of my life to keep the adrenaline flowing. I don't want to be pinned down.

The regulars usually leave by around ten thirty. Before the early lunchtime rush, I take a break and stand in the kitchen sipping a hot espresso. The hit of caffeine wakes my senses. I close my eyes. I remember my first day here, the scent of coffee, the buzz of customers, the mouth-watering cakes. Now, I fail to notice new tortes and my taste buds favour savoury. Coffee is still important.

Franz is working with me today. He's not often out of the kitchen and is usually busy making a lot of the cakes. He nips my thigh as he passes. I'd find it offensive if it was any other man. 'So, what's with Hans?' he asks.

'What do you mean?' I put the cup down and stare at him.

He shrugs, 'I don't know, you know. He's just a bit ...off, or something.'

'Right.' I don't know what to say.

'Haven't you noticed? He seems edgy.'

'He's always edgy.'

'Not like this.' Franz leans in towards a carton of milk and screws his nose up. 'Off, I think. Here.' He thrusts it towards me.

'Fine, I trust your judgement.'

'I'll throw it.'

'Your choice,' I say.

'So what do you know about him? Do you like him?'

'I don't mind working with him but I wouldn't want him to get close.'

Franz is emptying the carton into the sink. 'I thought we checked these.'

'You just did,' I say.

'No. Properly check it, before I use it.'

'Right. What do you think of Hans?' I ask him.

'Don't much like the guy. He seems too smooth, too confident. And he knows everything. Well, that's how it comes across. He's not very natural, is he?'

'I don't think so, but everyone else loves him. I keep a distance.'

Franz turns the tap off and looks up. 'They're nice to his face but I heard some of the other girls saying he was too flirty and they've heard him saying different things to different people. Word is he hasn't been to Graz at all. He's all talk and charm.'

'So where did he go?'

'Don't know,' says Franz. 'I think he's been trained in London. Alice heard him when he was drunk one night. Talked about finding stolen art.'

'What?'

'Art. You know? Tracking down lost paintings. Detective stuff.'

I can hear my heartbeat. I have to get out, figure out what to do. I need to think fast. 'Franz, can you tell the boss I'm not feeling well. I'm going home.'

He wipes his hands on a towel, eyebrows raised, hair falling across his face. 'All right. Are we good? Everything OK?'

'Yes. I can feel a migraine coming on.'

'You don't get migraines.'

'Can you just tell him?'

He nods. 'You would tell me if you were in trouble or something?'

'Of course. Don't worry. I'll be fine. See you tomorrow.' I lean in towards him, put a hand on his shoulder, squeeze gently and I turn to go to the back room to take off my uniform. I feel my cheeks flush, which is unusual. My head is fine, but I have to get out. I hang up the tunic, grab my bag and walk down the stairs. I clutch my chest as I reach the street. Why would he tell me he went to Graz? And if he didn't go, what was he doing in London? The only place linked to stolen art is the Art Loss Register. They wouldn't have trained him. The Art Loss Register prevents the handling of stolen art through database searches, they report and register the stolen pieces and recover work, using specialist teams. The FBI have a National Stolen Art File database and investigate organised crime, but they're based in the States. Unless he worked for a crime squad. I can't figure out what kind of training he would have received, or whether the story is even true.

The breeze on my cheeks reminds me how stifling it is trapped inside a building. I don't like being contained in the same space for too long. I crave the city air. The gallery is the most suffocating space although the thrill of being

152

surrounded by paintings outweighs my neuroses. The windows are usually open during lectures, keeping me awake, and there's good reason to fall asleep in some of the lectures.

I have to see Maria. I wonder what she might know about Hans. For the first time, I feel out of the loop and wonder if I ever had control. The job is addictive, but I'm starting to feel real fear. I have to press on, push through it, return the works. I have to outsmart Albert and, maybe now, Herr Schneider, to get the paintings back to their original owners. I imagine flames engulfing the canvases and soldiers laughing like a pack of hyenas.

I arrive at Schönbrunn, the sun beating down on the yellow apartment buildings, a glow that only comes with sunset. Temperatures have dropped from the mid-summer highs of forty-three degrees but the heat is still enough to disrupt the day. There are beads of perspiration on my neck. I slide the bag from my shoulder to allow my skin to breathe and notice Maria's curtain fall loose as I cross the road from the station. She has been watching, waiting. The door opens and her face appears.

'Liesl, how nice to see you. Hot, isn't it?'

'The summers always catch me off guard. Could I have a glass of water?'

'Of course. Come in, sit down.'

I think of Herr Schneider's last question. Why would I remember what his brother was wearing? How does he know that I found his body? Why did Albert send me to Schneider's brother? The mystery of the body in the apartment is still on my mind. Am I working for Albert? Schneider? Someone else?

'Maria, can I ask you something?'

'Of course, dear. What is it?' I find the term, *dear*, irritating. She passes me a biscuit and pours a cup of coffee. I add some cream and nestle the cup in the palms of my hands, despite the heat.

'When I went to Herr Schneider's house, he knew it was me who found his brother's body.'

'His brother?'

'Yes, didn't you know?'

'Who is his brother? You've lost me.'

'The body at the station? It was his brother.' Her eyes widen. She rests her cup down on the table without pouring the cream, leans in towards me, stares into my eyes.

'The body with the note and the brooch?' she asks. I nod. 'Why? Why would Albert send you to his brother if he knew?'

'That's what I don't understand. They didn't have a good relationship. He didn't show any emotion when we talked about him. He was more concerned with the note and whether there was anything else on his body.'

Maria leans in further. 'And what did you say? This isn't good.' She shakes her head.

'I didn't know what to say. I told him there was just the note, but I'm afraid he knows I took the brooch.'

'Liesl, Albert has put you in dangerous situations. I hear Herr Schneider has contacts in Berlin. From what I've heard, he was a Nazi sympathiser. I wouldn't be surprised if you find out he has links to the art you are trying to recover. Be careful.'

'He has Klimt originals hanging in his hallway. Sketches,' I say.

'Why would he hang them in view?'

'That's exactly what I wondered. He seemed keen for me to notice.'

'Liesl,' her eyes widen. 'I know a man in Berlin, a dealer. He might be able to help. He battled to survive during the early forties. You can trust him.' She reaches down into the fabric box by her chair which is stuffed with folded newspapers, the inside pages turned out, half read. Her fingers feel their way into one of the inside pockets and she pulls out an address book. She thumbs her way through the pages until she reaches the middle.

'Knaus,' she says. 'Peter Knaus. He specialises in Picassos. The Führer hated them, of course. Knaus hid them away so that they would not be destroyed. He might be able to tell you more.'

'Thank you,' I say. I can't help noticing a sadness in her eyes as she tucks the address book back, as though burying a part of her life.

'Liesl, I know it must be difficult to understand, but it was a painful time for those who loved art and culture, those who cherished the works that were lost. The newspapers only covered the political changes, land occupation, leadership, that sort of thing, but art was all some of us knew and taking it away was like removing oxygen from the air.' She looks out of the window, gazes into the distance. 'The fact that families were torn from their homes was only ever a part of the story. The pain for many was in leaving their cultural heritage, the great works handed down through generations, many holding memories of portraits hung on the walls of grandparents' homes. It wasn't just the monetary value, it was these memories. They stole memories which held the very essence of family life and which held stories about the people and about the paintings.' She clasps her hand over her lips and hands me the number.

'Thank you, Maria. Thank you.' We drink coffee in silence. There are no words that will comfort her, not for something like this. It's not really my forte, either. I hear the sound of coaches as they park outside and unload crowds of tourists. We are used to seeing foreign visitors rolling off coaches in shorts and t-shirts with single-lens reflex cameras draped around their necks. Vienna guide books crumpled at the edges and pushed into pockets, anticipation in their eyes. I hear the click of the cameras. Maria smiles as I look up. I look again at the photographs of her family. 'You must miss them,' I say, aware that this can't match the gravity of her loss.

She nods. 'I do, but I have to let the past go. You can't be bitter. Holding on to a wrongdoing only drives a knife into your own soul. You push and twist until you bleed dry. You have to forgive, Liesl. Anger doesn't hurt the perpetrators. I refuse to see myself as a victim. When I knew that you could retrieve some of the art, I felt a sense of justice. I admire you, Liesl, I really do, but don't expect the journey to be smooth. And you need to think about the other work you do. You have been following the orders of a corrupt man.'

'If I stop now it will make Albert suspicious. I have to keep moving and work the two alongside each other until I can pull out. If he finds out, I'll be dead.'

'Yes, of course.' She knows the danger.

'I've already been attacked and I might have been the body in the apartment or at Stephansplatz.' I get up and walk towards the door. She follows close behind.

'Make sure you contact Peter Knaus. I'm sure he can give

you some information that will help.' She clasps my hand as I leave and closes the door swiftly, but I know her eyes are still on me.

Chapter 25

I jump off the tram outside the Belvedere. It's only 9 am.
There are fewer guards earlier in the day. The sunlight catches
the statues surrounding the palace roof. I cross the road and
head in through the main gates, lions above the wrought
iron watch those who enter and exit. The gardens are a
sweeping display of greens, reds and yellows. The Lower
Belvedere lies in the shade with its cascading, tiered fountains,
the roof casting long shadows across the path. This is the
most serene of Vienna's palace buildings. Latticed roof
patterns and oval-shaped scenes of the life of Apollo are
reminiscent of the life of Prince Eugene. I enjoy the city at
this time of year; the low, early morning light and the scent
of bloom, without the bustle of tourists. There are fewer
here in late summer than before the Christmas markets begin.
July and August are almost void of locals, most favouring
the cool mountain air. My work keeps me here in the city.

I slip in through the entrance and wait until the woman
at the desk is distracted before making my way up the marble
staircase. Statues watch me from behind, possibly aware of
the theft about to take place. I glance at the expanse of
water in the gardens behind the palace. I should feel fear,
but I no longer feel anything. I turn my back towards the
entrance and notice the guard walking towards the shop to
the right hand side. I make my way to the first floor and
drift through the Klimts with an irreverent ease. Viewers in

the gallery linger by each piece with obvious appreciation. I don't have time for this. Instead, I find the Klimt Albert has requested and slide it off the wall and out of the frame. It becomes easier each time. I take it to the lift with my coat thrown over the front. This gallery is smaller, making an operation like this more difficult. I think about the numerous paintings I need to return to their owners. Fulfilling Albert's wishes frustrates me now. I'm wasting time but I have no choice. He'd become suspicious if I suddenly stopped following orders. I already have Schneider on my case.

'Morning.' A visitor nods as he passes.

I nod and keep moving. He probably thinks I work here. I'm moving too fast to view the paintings. I press the button but the lift continues to the first floor without stopping. I feel tense. I wait for it to come back down. The ropes stop moving and start up again. The number one flashes on the screen as it reaches my level. The doors open, I step in, and breathe out slowly as they close behind me.

Be careful. Maria's words replay. The note telling me to leave the city warned me to be careful. The notes can't have been from Maria. I'm sure I can trust her. They could be from anyone. Albert may not even exist. I have to pretend that nothing's changed. I have to get the art back into the hands of their rightful owners but for now, I must get this painting to the dead drop in the library. Albert asked me to drop it in the map section. I'll get a taxi instead of the tram. It's less obvious and safer for now. The driver offers to put my 'parcel' in the boot, although all he can see is the coat draped over it. I shake my head, clutch it tighter, bow my head and slip into the back seat.

'Library, please,' I say, avoiding eye contact. I've already put on my sunglasses. I don't want him to remember my face. The thud of the base from the radio stills my thoughts.

The driver pulls up outside the library. I hand him more than the fee and wave my hand. He can keep the change. Without looking at him, I get out of the taxi, clutching the painting. I race down a side alley and tear the painting off its frame. I'm beginning to loathe this part. I can see the horror of the risks involved and I wince as I take off the last corner. I look both ways and discard the frame in a large bin, then roll the canvas up and into my bag. For the first time, I feel disgusted with myself for what I do, and that it's become second nature. I have no idea where this one is going. I never do, but this time it matters.

I should go into the library and follow instructions to leave it in the map section but I can't. I see Martha's face as I gave her the painting in the park. On that morning in Stadtpark, I felt a rare sense of doing something right. It was a strange sensation and replaced the shame I feel each morning when I enter the side chapel in the cathedral, knowing something's not right, that I took a wrong turn somewhere and can never turn back. Sometimes, Omama had said, you have to take a path into darkness before you are pushed to find the light. When I was a girl, I'd climbed into a tunnel, my curiosity drawing me further in, taking turnings I could never remember until I couldn't find my way out. The light had vanished and I hadn't noticed the darkness. I wonder if this is what she meant. I know I lost sight of daylight long ago. The darkness has always felt familiar, but since that day in Albert's apartment, and then in Maria's, it feels less comfortable.

I walk in the direction of the cathedral, turn right along Fleischmarkt and left into Laurenzergasse. The police station is on the right, before the Danube. I reach the entrance, pull the painting from my bag and leave it on the doorstep. I feel relieved as I walk away. There are no cameras that I can see, but I've pulled my hat down over my eyes and turned up my jacket collar. I keep my head down and walk swiftly to Swedenplatz, then wait for the next tram. I get on and find a seat at the back. I imagine the taste of vodka in the back of my throat in anticipation of the glass I'll pour when I reach the apartment. Narrowly missing my stop, I jump off before it pulls away and disappears into the haze of the street. I turn the key in the main entrance door and head up the spiral stone staircase. Reaching my apartment door, I put the smaller key into the lock and turn the key only once. The door opens. I should be able to turn it twice. I re-lock the door, then turn the key again. Once. Twice. I've checked it carefully every morning since the disturbance. The kitchen looks undisturbed but my mug sits in the sink. I left it on the draining board. A second mug is in the sink next to it. I touch the coffee jug. It's still warm but switched off. Someone's turned on the machine and made themselves at home. There's a sound in the living room. I walk slowly towards the door. Papers are strewn across the sofa. The windows are closed and the radio is playing. Whoever disturbed the apartment helped themselves to my coffee and radio.

A quick check of the bathroom and bedroom shows that the apartment is now empty. I pour a vodka and knock it back, clear the papers, slump onto the sofa and light a cigarette. There's one left and I toss the empty pack onto the floor. It lands on top of the papers. I'd usually put it neatly on the table. The words *Smoking can kill,* emblazoned across the packet sit neatly on top of the information about the burnt artworks that didn't survive. I walk over to the window and struggle to lift it up. Something is jammed into the frame. I pull, and a piece of folded card drops out. The window shoots up. I pick up the card, flip it over and toss it onto the pile of paper on the floor. Smoke fills my lungs, my fingertips tingle. I look back at the pile of papers, the empty Memphis packet and the folded card. I'll be dead before I figure out who wedged it into the window frame. Dead.

Chapter 26

I rub one foot over the other, a movement that soothes my nerves. The rucksack on my wardrobe is easy to reach and it lands with a thud on my mattress. The straps are worn, but it still holds together. I throw in enough clothes for a week or two and gather up my wash things from the bathroom: a toothbrush, toothpaste, a fresh tube of shower gel, a razor and a flannel. Inside the cabinet above the sink I find painkillers. Sleeping pills go into the side pocket, just in case. I don't take them every night. The doctor prescribed them when I was too stressed to sleep after Oma died. It was easier than seeing someone. It works faster than alcohol, although less enjoyable. The effects lasted longer but not so long that I couldn't function the next day. Don't get hooked, he said. So I only take them when I really need them. I took one last night.

I watch my hands shake as I turn on the tap. I hold them out and try to keep them still but I see my fingers jumping like salmon swimming upstream. I cup them under the cold water and splash my face. It's cold enough to cause a shock of pain, but it feels good. Nothing else feels good at the moment. I remember Maya's face when I handed over the painting, forcing me to keep moving. I pull the drawstring, throw the bag into the case, go over to the antique cabinet with the clear bottles and open a fresh one. This one's a Jura Whisky, bought in Edinburgh a few years ago. The flavour's clean and sharp. It burns at the back of my throat. I tip my head up and swallow.

The train to Berlin should get me in at 7:20am with a change at Mannheim. I can sleep for a few hours first. I pick up the papers, throw the cigarette packet in the bin, the words *Smoking can kill* still facing me, refusing to turn away. I lift up the rug in the living room, wrench the floorboard free and slide the papers into the darkness between the beams. The board and rug fall back into place and I wonder, for a moment, where I would hide, if I had to. There's no place that would accommodate an adult body, only some papers and a few paintings, items thin enough to disappear.

I turn off the radio, half draw the curtains, and take one last look around the apartment before stepping outside and closing the door behind me. The lock turns. Once. Twice. I turn back to look at the door as I reach the stairs, then head down with my backpack slung over one shoulder. I feel its lightness compared to the weight of the canvases and relief that I'm not carrying anything of value. Warm air rises up from the cool stone steps and caresses my face, reminding me of stepping off a plane onto hot tarmac.

I reach Westbahnhof from the U3 line on the underground and stand in the entrance hall with other travellers, gazing up at the screens. The 10:52pm leaves from platform 8 in an hour. I take the escalators to the upper level to find caffeine and a paper. The station reminds me of an airport: the trails of baggage, the searching expressions in people's eyes and the hum of announcements – arrivals, departures, rare delays. We pride ourselves on our punctuality. Anything longer than two minutes is deemed late. The escalator is short, bringing me up to a level where I can lean over the glass barrier and watch passengers scurrying across the oversized, colourless floor tiles. They all enter and exit through sets of double doors labelled Eingang or Ausgang, ants following one another back to their nests, some carrying food, others carrying nothing, none deviating from the path: entrance to platform, exit to road. I look up at the clock. The black flecks where the numbers should be frustrate me when I'm tired or on the move. They look like lost ants that have congregated around a morsel of food, fixed until they're free to leave. Instead, the hands turn almost invisibly, minutes overtaking hours and slipping into the past.

The café is empty. Posters of unrecognisable jazz musicians plastered across brick walls are torn and peeled, rebelliously refusing to stick. The light above me flickers as the rain strikes the roof. I hear thunder rolling across the sky, lightning flashes against the glass panels high up on the side walls. I order an espresso and a strudel. I have a long night ahead of me, unless I sleep. The aroma of coffee is comforting. A ruffled pile of papers lies sprawled across the counter. I sift through them until I reach a *Der Standard*, then tuck it under my arm and dig out some coins. I find a table in the back corner and drop the backpack on the chair next to me. It feels too light for the size, but I haven't packed it full, only enough for a few days. The front page of the paper doesn't hold my interest but I catch a glimpse of a face on page ten, the body, Herr Schneider's brother. His face is instantly recognisable. I skim the words, but they don't register. Then, I discover that he had a sister. I squint at the black ink in the dull light in the café until the words align. I see a face. It's Maria. Why didn't she tell me she had two brothers? I stole a brooch from the body of one. The other is threatening me with charges of manslaughter. She knows all of this. Maybe she's unaware of any siblings.

'Are you all right, Miss?' The waitress puts an espresso down on the table. 'You look pale. Sugar?'

'No. I'm fine. No sugar.' I wave away the sugar pot and turn my face back towards the headlines. She returns to reloading the croissants onto the display counter, glancing at me a few times before disappearing. I stare at the plait resting on the nape of Maria's neck and wonder how her brother was killed. There were no marks on the body that I could identify. The word 'drunk' sounds so terse when I think about it, cruel and devoid of emotion. Maybe he was sober. Maybe he wasn't a drunk. Nobody seems to know anything about the man. Even his own brother had no words to share. It's as though he never existed.

I read past the headline to the paragraph describing Maria and Herr Schneider as his siblings. It says that their parents died and I wonder if that's what fractured their relationships, and if it might be the reason why Herr Schneider spoke about the body with such disdain, but I'm sure there's more. Maria talked about her parents but never mentioned siblings.

I take a sip of the coffee. It burns. The waitress returns with a steaming slice of strudel and a generous helping of cream. I cut into the flesh of the apple with a cake fork, cream runs down over the pastry. I lift the fork to my mouth and close my eyes. This is the first food I've eaten in almost twenty-four hours. I check my pocket for a lighter and leave half a pack of cigarettes on the table for later. The waitress watches me. She empties the shelves of torte and croissants which I imagine are now dried at the edges, and replaces them with fresher ones. Everything will have been out since the early hours.

I read the rest of the article. It says that they were estranged from each other, but doesn't give a reason. I think back to

Herr Schneider's disinterest when we discussed the body. And Maria? How was it that on the many occasions that we discussed both brothers, she revealed nothing of her connection with either of them? They weren't among the family photographs on her shelf, only her parents and grandparents. She told me that she was an only child. It was a lie.

I put the paper down, place the cup of coffee on top, then remove the cup in case I need the evidence. I pull a cigarette out of the pack, flip the lighter, draw in the nicotine and feel my nerves settle. The waitress is pouring herself a coffee. I imagine it's been a long shift and she's glad the café is empty of customers and clatter.

I pick up the paper and slip through the pages until I reach an article on the art stored in Berlin and Munich. Images of Monets, Cezannes and Mondrians are splashed across a double page. The article says something about the injustice of the looting and that experts in America and Israel are in talks with the collectors and the owners as they try to relocate the art and get the pieces back to the families. This, against my own operations, feels like a huge feat. It's difficult to imagine how it will all be returned. I still believe that museums have no superior right over an individual to art, especially not if it's stolen. Omama always told me that my words were harsh, but it's honesty. You can cover up theft and call it movement of property but it's still misappropriation in its worst form. I shudder to think of the works I've moved for Albert, or whoever is sending the letters. Theft: that's what it is. I am a thief. Now, I have to bring some form of restoration by returning the most unlawful of losses. The Jewish art that was plundered is unforgivable. This could be a war crime.

"It is not the mission of art to wallow in filth." According to the article, the words of the Führer had been plastered across walls. He didn't like the way that men and women were represented by artists like Picasso, Kokoschka or Kandinsky. I wonder how strong he really felt, and whether his anger, in fact, stemmed from a lack of strength. I know that my hard-headed approach to life comes from a vulnerability that no one sees. There's a dragon in all our hearts. Some are able to tame it or turn it away and welcome a lighter animal – an eagle, perhaps, or a dove – while others destroy everything around them, quenching the very fire of life.

People criticise these monsters but history repeats itself through other wars, in other lands, ricocheting from one place to another. Anger, and the search for domination and ethnic purity are dressed up as righteousness and justification, but it's an arrogance that doesn't understand that we are similar creatures. We all crave safety, identity and purpose. We all want to lay down our heads at night knowing that we'll wake to stability, that our loved ones are not at risk of harm, that we can go about our day with freedom of choice.

The article in the paper cites the words painted across the walls of the 'Degenerate art exhibition' in Munich in November of 1937: *20,000 people a day came to see 650 works of art confiscated from German museums. An insult to German womanhood*, reads one slogan. *Deliberate sabotage of national defence*, says another. My stomach turns. I stub out the cigarette in an ashtray, place the coffee back on the table, take a gulp of water and breathe out as though exorcising evil. *Madness becomes method* is the last line I read before closing the paper. I want to throw it into the bin by the door but, with the article about Maria and her siblings, I decide against discarding the information.

Chapter 27

The station clock reaches 9:35pm. I stub out the rest of the cigarette and go to the counter with ten euros. The waitress watches me leave. Without waiting for the change, I make my way down to platform eight. The train is resting almost against the buffers and I climb into a carriage towards the end. The seats are reasonably empty. It's not a popular time to travel. I pull out a bottle of water and a book, and set the rucksack down and allow myself the luxury of an extra seat. An elderly man is sitting adjacent to me across the aisle, looking out of the window at other trains waiting at the station, watching passengers scurrying up and down the platform with wheeled suitcases and travel backpacks like mine. He looks sad or hopeful. I can't tell which of the two. His forehead is furrowed, eyebrows lowered, sheltering his eyes from the sunlight, or from life. He has what looks like a picnic hamper on the floor by his seat with a flask pushing through at the top, its silver coating dulled with age to a weary grey. His body and belongings use an economy of space I cannot imitate. He looks at his watch and up at the station clock hoping, I assume, that they will match up. The latter tells him that the train will depart in two minutes.

Only his eyes swivel up and back down and rest on a woman who is taking off her cardigan and stuffing it into a bag. Her shoulders are toned and bronzed. He is still watching her as she walks towards the back of the train and I wonder if he has a wife or if he is alone and on his way to meet someone. I imagine his life, all neatly folded away into cupboards and his kitchen, dark and filled with an assortment of teas and china cups with roses and gold leaf and a biscuit tin just out of reach. He looks about Maria's age, maybe younger, but his expression is fixed by years of pain, his eyes dark and marred by disappointment. I feel these things when I look at people, flashes of a life lived with loss or regret. Sometimes the eyes are bright and hopeful. He doesn't look hopeful, his mouth turning down at the corners. He soothes himself by stroking a few fingers across each hand in a repetitive motion that I have seen in small children and trauma survivors.

The station master shouts an order and the doors close. I fail to hear the sentences, the endings swallowed up in the bell of the tannoy. The words roll through the metal, morphing into something completely unrecognisable, as though we are submerged under water. Others, I notice, ignore them too, preferring to trust their instincts, or to look at a clock or a timetable. It seems pointless to stand there and shout something no one attends to except maybe the driver. If he is the only person who needs to know, then the job is done. We pick up speed as the train rolls into the open, leaving a latent orange haze of station lights, and the din of train announcements, plunging us into the blackness of the Vienna night. I pick up my book and run my fingers over the front cover. A lone woman walking up a rock-covered hill towards a small, concrete house, is overlaid by large brown lettering: The Keeper of Books by J.A. Cooper. The author is unknown to me, but I bought it under the auspices of her being a prize-winning travel journalist who works in Human Rights. The scent of the paper is comforting.

I bought it at the second hand bookshop, the inside front pages scrawled with notes and a message, *To Susanne with love from Bernard. You will always be my muse.* The price is pencilled in at the top right hand corner. I bought it for a mere eighty-five cents. I can't imagine being anyone's muse. The thought feels stifling. The scent of old paper is pungent, the lignin releasing itself like campfire smoke.

I sink into the seat and read the back cover. It's non-fiction about a journalist working in Kabul. As I read on, it's more poetic than much of the recent fiction I've read. There's little time to read, so I savour these hours ahead where nothing else pulls at me. She plants us into a scene with immediate tension; the father is considering taking another wife and the children are afraid of his anger. The wife is silent and I fear for her safety. Without knowing anything about her life, or even her name, I already want to protect her from him, from his words and his hands. The skill of a good writer lies in the ability to put you into a scene and hold you there, playing with your emotions until they decide to release you and move you into another scene, a cat teasing a mouse before going in for the kill. The tension ebbs and flows through the first chapter and I pause to drink some water and scan the view, but outside is black. We're heading north from the centre and there are no towns or villages to light our way. The man on the seat across from me is asleep with an empty paper bag beside him and an open flask. I can smell chicken soup and home-made bread. His hands are rough and calloused.

I draw my knees up to my chest and wrap a fleece across my legs. The windows are open a chink and the night air is cold. I could close them, but then I'd feel suffocated. The faint scent of pickled gherkins will only become stronger until we disembark at Mannheim. A mature stilton or a pickled vegetable, neither should be left open for longer than is necessary.

Cooper writes about the matchbox houses crammed into the landscape, telegraph wires stretching up over the mountain like ski lifts. She describes the craggy mountainside and the turquoise domes of mosques rising through mists. Bazaars bustle with children and market-sellers. She draws us back to the husband, who is still speaking, but she does not mention the wife for a few pages. I wonder if this is deliberate; the unseen member of the family. The children are afraid. The other woman walks. She is a villager. They recognise her immediately and she's a good deal younger than their mother. I close the book and pull out a cigarette and a lighter. The tension on the pages is too much. There's enough tension in my own life. I don't need to be drawn into anyone else's. I walk to the end of the carriage, taking my purse and house keys. The window is ajar and I pull it wide open. The lighter fails to ignite. A man passes me in the corridor, takes the lighter and ignites it with one deft thumb movement. I nod to thank him, but he's already walked into the next carriage where my rucksack lies on the seat and the man is sleeping with his basket and flask. For a second, I feel uncomfortable, a chill at my back, and I peer through the window. He is no longer visible. His manner was strange, forceful. I don't remember anyone offering to light a cigarette for me. In fact it wasn't an offer, more an assumption.

I watch the lights from distant towns flicker and vanish. The blackness of the sky is at last lifted by dull moonlight. The only sound is the train's wheels against the tracks. My body judders as the carriages pull against each other. I think about Maria's words and wonder why she's led me to Herr Knaus, and whether this is a decoy. I've trusted her so far, but the terrain keeps shifting, sand dunes moved by the wind. Schneider, Albert and Hans have all changed and become three siblings. There are two bodies and various pieces of stolen art to understand. I hope that this Peter Knaus is an honest man. I need someone to tell me the truth.

I remember watching Opa painting and Omama walking into the room with an ashen face and eyes wide open. I didn't know then that I would never see Mother and Father again. I don't remember much beyond their eyes meeting and him leaving the room as she spoke. I remember the smell of the oil paints and the half empty canvas with its streaks of background colour. I remember sitting on the wooden floor boards holding my doll. Her name was Anna. She went everywhere with me and was the only constant in my life that I could remember. Her hair was made of red wool, and she wore a brown patterned dress. Her eyes were blue and remained fixed in a startled expression. The fabric was soft and smelled of Mother. They were the only scents I could remember for a long time: the smell of Omama's perfume and Opa's oils.

The cigarette glows, the stub shortened to my fingertips. I throw it onto the tracks and return to my carriage where the lights are lowered to a nighttime glow. The other passenger remains asleep as I take my place next to the window and pick up the book, flipping to the last page. Hans once told me he always reads the last sentence before starting a new book. We'd argued about it spoiling the story. I'm not planning to finish it this evening so reading the ending will do no harm. I turn to the last page, skim the acknowledgements and the list of the other books by the same publisher, until I reach the empty pages and the last page of the story. I decide against reading the last line and go back to the beginning. Why would anyone want to know the ending? I want to feel the characters and the city. I want to smell the fires and the dust. I need to be in the shoes of the character or the narrator who, in this instance, is the youngest daughter. She's fearful of her father arranging a marriage with a boy in the next town. I can identify with her sense of fear of the unknown. It's why we read, to find ourselves. The mother has left the home to find firewood and the father is looking longingly at the new woman. My stomach twists. The eldest daughter is already married and living nearby. She makes tea. All eyes are on him, a man whose every whim is catered for by the women in the house.

I close the book, knowing that my mind should be open to different cultures and ways of doing things, but the treatment of the women in this book, as commodities to be owned and traded, disgusts me. I don't care to indulge in any further details, convinced I've already read enough. I finish the water and look over at the sleeping man. His head has dropped onto his left shoulder, threatening to pull him over to the next seat where he would crush only the empty paper bag.

Chapter 28

I wake somewhere towards Mannheim and go in search of a coffee. My fellow passenger has left the carriage leaving behind his paper, tired and curled at the edges, which is how I now feel. I pick it up on the way to the restaurant car. I can smell fruit tea and hope they sell caffeinated drinks. The carriage is filled with smoke. It's too much, even for me. I pay for a black coffee and leave quickly, noticing the train's emptiness. We wait a while before the train pulls out of the station. A man who boarded the train at Mannheim is walking towards me from the next carriage. He stares at me through the glass and I look down, knowing in the pit of my stomach that he is here for me. I hear the handle turn, take a sip of coffee and open the paper. I avoid the temptation to hide my face behind the papers and look straight at him as he walks towards me. He's wearing dark glasses and the lower part of his face is wrapped in a scarf. Both are out of place on the train: it's too dark for sunglasses and too warm in the carriages for a scarf. I think of my gloved hands when I am on the job, and of my training to notice out of place objects and items of clothing. I feel sick. His face reveals nothing as he passes and reaches with one hand towards me. I don't move or look up. A letter lands between the paper and my body. He doesn't speak or stop. I turn and lean into the aisle. He is gone. The door at the end of the carriage slams as if shutting me out, telling me not to follow.

For a moment, I think of the man who attacked me on the way to the library, and the man who watched me leave Albert's and board the tram, and the many times when I felt I was being watched. It doesn't occur each week, but often enough. Most people are unaware of being followed, but after being attacked or if you're trained, you know straight away. I need to avoid the fear and paranoia that haunt me when I'm tired. It's risky to show nerves, even to those you trust. You can be deceived by the most innocent of people. Sometimes.

I fold the paper loosely and throw the empty water bottle into an adjacent bin. The letter feels heavy, the quality of the paper I presume, rather than the contents. I slide my finger into the seal. A sharp edge cuts my skin. I suck it and taste the sweetness. I manage to free the letter from the envelope. It's a typed note which looks unfamiliar. The style is different to Albert's and the ink is heavier. It gives no introduction, no name or greeting.

You're searching in the wrong place. Knaus won't tell you anything. Go back to Vienna and ask Herr Schneider more questions. Don't be afraid to find out about the body.

I fold the letter and replace it in the envelope. Why isn't this from Albert and why am I being told to ignore Knaus? The only person who knows my movements is Maria, unless I'm being followed. For one pair of feet on the ground there could be five pairs of eyes following. Surveillance is like an oak tree; you may only see the trunk, but underneath, below ground and firmly attached, are many roots. If I notice one person in the distance, especially if I am approached, which is rare, there may be seven or eight others researching my history and my moves. I think, for a moment, about my apartment and the disturbed items – the soap on the floor and the open window – and I shiver. I don't know how many people were involved: one, maybe three, unknown feet across my own floor, violating my personal space and possessions. It feels like a burglary but leaves a more menacing aftermath. I know this feeling. In the children's home where I stayed until Omama was well enough to take me, my space was not respected and my things were ransacked. A crow waits until the mother is gone before puncturing the sides of the shell and draining its contents.

The early morning sun floods Berlin station, casting shafts of light across an empty platform. I step on light and dark alternating across the concrete to the exit. The scent of coffee and crepes pulls me towards the nearest café and I order a black coffee and a croissant. I can't stomach the sugar in a crepe at this time of day and with little sleep. Having not had the time to clean my teeth, I take a mint before drinking the coffee. I hold my breath as I catch a glimpse of the man who walked through my carriage with the letter. He is leaving the station and moving swiftly. I want to follow him.

The German here is different, harder somehow, and my Viennese accent draws a quizzical look from the waitress. I wonder whether English might be preferable. She scowls when I fail to use the preferred 'Guten Tag' and responds to my 'Gruss Gott' with mild disdain. As I pick up my hot croissant, it deflates, leaving a flat pastry. The coffee restores me after a disturbed night. I drink a glass of water from the silver tray and drain the coffee cup. She raises her eyes as I get up to pay.

Peter Knaus' gallery is outside the central district, tucked away according to Maria, down a quiet backstreet with antique shops and a small bar. I find a map and a tram heading east from Alexanderplatz. The day looks overcast, clouds rolling in from the west. Berlin is a mix of vibrant modern architecture scattered across a canvas of soulless ex-communist blocks and run down shops with windows without colour or individuality. Glass fronted high-rise buildings house the centres of commerce. The government buildings and museums are regal. The city is a patchwork of greys and colours, the brighter segments forcing it into the twenty-first century and wiping over the past. Rulers and kingdoms have left their mark: Prussia, the German Empire and the Federal Republic, the Weimar Republic and Nazi Germany. I shudder. The Bellevue and Charlottenburg Palaces remind me of Vienna's Schönbrunn and Hofburg Palaces. The architecture in Berlin seems familiar but more mixed and dislocated. The Fernsehturm tower rises over other buildings, watching its inhabitants from a great height. The tram heads down Karl-Marx-Allee, lined with buildings from the Stalin era, heading east. The Stasi museum sits back and to my left, a reminder of the city's past. I can't imagine being trapped on the eastern side of the wall, separated from family members. I push aside thoughts of my parents. Images of my grandfather painting, then leaving the room, and me sitting on the wooden floor with my doll, return.

I get off at Fischerundfischer at Strausberger Platz and walk towards Mitte Gallery on Singerstrasse. I take a small side road immediately before the gallery and follow the map until I find Knaus's gallery set back from the road. You wouldn't know it was a gallery unless you knew what you were looking for. It's more like a second-hand book shop. I step in through a wood-framed glass door filled with books and antiques. The smell of old paper and dust hits me as I close the door behind me.

'Hello,' I call as I step further in. 'Hello.' But there is no reply. Floorboards creak above my head and an elderly man appears at the top of a flight of stairs, like a ghost, hovering, threatening to disappear from sight.

'Liesl,' he says, as though asking a question.

'Herr Knaus.'

A broad, unexpected grin stretches across his face. He walks down the stairs holding the rail tightly, supporting his frail frame with his left hand. His skin is dotted with sunspots and his eyes are a deep grey. His trousers would hang loose if it were not for the brown, leather braces which hold them up.

'Call me Peter,' he says, as he takes my hands. 'Dear girl, I've been waiting for you. Maria told me you would come.'

'She did?'

'Yes. Sit down.'

He leads me into the downstairs room. Dust flies off a covered stool which he pats as he passes. Particles spin in the light between half drawn curtains, dulling a third of the bookshelves. The shelves are covered with rugs and stacked with paintings, telescopes and compasses.

He looks at me and I see that he is pleased I came. I hope he'll be able to tell me why I'm here and something else that will fit the pieces together and make sense of them. Help me to understand the past.

Chapter 29

'Herr Knaus. Peter. What can you tell me about the stolen art?'

'It depends on what you want to know. Is it about the confiscated art?' His smile disappears.

'Yes.' I feel uncomfortable, knowing this will be difficult for him, but I have to ask.

'Go ahead,' he says, closing his eyes, perhaps transporting himself back a few painful decades.

'Is it true that you collected art that was being confiscated? Modern art? Picassos? Klees?'

He nods in a way that could almost be missed. 'Yes. They were destroying them. Someone had to stop them. I risked imprisonment and possibly my life, but these pieces are our history.' He makes a fist with his right hand, swings it up towards his chest. 'They are priceless. He called it degenerative art. He was a monster. They were ordered to burn the paintings and dispose of them like animals thrown out onto the streets. He didn't even get into Art College. They had the good sense to turn him down. In my view, the man simply couldn't paint. His revenge? An exhibition of his *degenerate* art in Dresden. Rotten, totally rotten. His bitterness brewed over time. Hate. It destroys people, chews them up ...'

His words drift into a silence that I don't want to break. I might shatter the moment with a thoughtless comment or an ignorant question. I've been part of the damage, moving paintings from galleries to collectors, possibly paintings once confiscated from Jewish owners. I'm part of this betrayal. I think of my cathedral visits each morning, my own hypocrisy. His distress is palpable. I remind myself that he answered my letter and invited me to Berlin. He must have a reason.

'Can I ask how you managed to get hold of the pieces?' I ask.

'I had people like you, Liesl, people who were willing and whom I paid to take that risk. They bought paintings from galleries in Munich and Dresden and stole from storage facilities. The thefts were purely for preservation. They would have been destroyed. We paid for what we could.'

I realise that Maria's told him about my own work and I feel exposed. 'How?' I ask.

He pauses before answering. 'I came from a wealthy family and I inherited a great deal. I was always taught that to whom much is given, much will be required in return. I had a friend, a fellow dealer and art historian in Munich who arranged sales and transfers, mainly via Switzerland. We knew a network of dealers. That was all.'

He looks too shabby and slow for this kind of operation and it's hard to imagine him coming from a wealthy family.

'What was his name?' I ask.

'Schneider. Herr Schneider. Nasty man, in my opinion. Opportunistic and hard hearted. Never liked him.'

'Where was he from?' I struggle to ask.

'He now lives in Vienna in a house on Billrothstrasse. Killed his brother, last I heard.'

'How do you know? That he killed his brother, I mean? Can you be sure?' I am shaking, but his eyes are on the wooden floor.

He detects my curiosity and he looks up. 'A friend told me.'

'Why would he kill his brother? Was there a threat?'

Peter shrugs his shoulders, a nonchalant act that tells me he doesn't care, only that he cared for the art and its safekeeping, not the man. 'I heard his brother was about to expose their past, but no one really knows. The police don't know. So you don't know anything. Understand me? Do you understand me Liesl?'

The second time he says this, his voice is insistent and his manner doesn't fit the weak frame of the man sitting in front of me. I clasp my shaking hands.

'Yes,' I say, 'yes I understand. Of course, I won't say anything. Who would I tell?'

'Maria? The police? I don't know, but I shouldn't even be talking to you,' he says, as though extricating himself from something unspeakable. 'Guilt has a strange way of finding its way out, doesn't it?

I stand up and walk around the room, avoiding an answer. 'These are beautiful. Have you always collected things? Art? Books?'

'Yes. I began as a boy with a stamp collection. It grew to postcards and ornaments. Then my father took me to a gallery in Berlin. He lost me in the Picasso section. I'd never seen anything like it – the imagination, the risk taking, the shape and form. I was hooked.'

'Do you have a wife? Family?'

He shakes his head. 'No, my wife was taken by the SS guards. We never had children. It's just me now. I met her in a gallery and I knew I would marry her the moment I saw her staring at a Picasso. She had long, dark hair and piercing eyes. She could light up a room with her words.

She knew how to bring people into conversation and she always looked for those who were on the fringe. I loved her. I remember the day I heard that she was gone. I was standing by the Brandenburg Gate waiting for someone. I held on to hope and I tried to contact people who might know, but I had to be careful. It broke my heart. These ...' he says, pointing across the room to the paintings,' I'd give all of these and everything I own to see her face.' His voice weakens.

'I'm so sorry.'

'Well, enough about me. Can I get you anything?'

'No,' I say. 'I'm fine. It was a long journey but I'm here. Maria thought we should meet.'

'How much do you know about her?' he asks.

'Only as much as she's told me, that her family died, she's related to the Hapsburgs and that she doesn't trust many people.'

'My wife was a friend of hers. When they took her, Maria came to visit me. She was heartbroken too. We've kept in touch. She kept my hopes up, but I think I knew then that I'd never see my wife again. Maria would have been in the public eye if she hadn't married the soldier. I think she preferred it that way, to bow out quietly, to live as normal a life as possible. She never needed the attention. I've always had realistic expectations of life so I'm rarely taken by surprise, but you surprise me. Liesl. I hope you don't mind me saying so.'

'What did you expect?' He doesn't know who I am or what I am.

'You're tougher than I had anticipated and more challenging. I expected someone darker, less direct. Don't take offence. It's actually quite refreshing.'

I notice the books on his top shelf are in alphabetical

order and there's a neatness behind the dust. I try to keep the conversation on track. I wonder whether he is deliberately deflecting my questions.

'So, this Herr Schneider,' I say.

'Do you know him?' he says.

'No, tell me more about him. Why would he kill his brother and what is his connection to the stolen art?' I think about the Klimt sketches on his wall and Peter's story makes sense.

'He had connections on both sides, but people say that he idolised the Führer. Never showed it, but thought the idea of racial purity and the purging of degenerate art were worth working towards. I believe the one led to the other.'

'In what way?'

'He began by humiliating the artists and went on to persecute people. He helped to set up the Degenerate Art Exhibition, the *Entartete Kunst*. I remember it well. It was a cold Munich winter. The exhibition ran from July to November and I went in the last month. Entry was free and the paintings looked like they had been thrown at the wall. I remember wanting to straighten a tilted Mondrian. We could have been viewing badly behaved animals at the zoo with signs reading *Danger, do not feed the monkeys*. It disgusted me, and others, but we kept quiet. Confrontation was too much of a risk, so many of us set up counter operations. We found out where the paintings were being sold and where they were stored. We bought. We stole. We did everything possible to rescue those works. Schneider could switch sides in a flash. Like a chameleon of the art world, he blended into any scene. I suppose I should admire him, but it's impossible. I've heard different things from people on both sides. I know a lot of dealers and experts in the trade. There were many grapevines. In those days it was all rumour and hearsay. I kept my head down but I listened. You always listened. He wasn't a good man, not from what I heard.'

'And you really think he killed his brother?' I ask. My stomach twists as I remember walking from the body straight into the cathedral, as though nothing had happened, wondering if I would be next.

'Yes. To be honest, having met the man, it didn't much surprise me,' he says. 'Military training.'

'Military?'

'Yes, after national service. I know no more than that.'

How could he kill his brother in broad daylight? And why the note told me not to speak to Peter Knaus. Was it from Schneider? Would he be following my tracks? I'm drawn to Peter's vodka collection in the corner of the room and try to avoid glancing at the bottles. I wish I was back in my apartment, in my own silent space.

His eyes are on me.

'Would you like a drink?' he asks.

'No, I'll wait until this evening,' I say, swiftly.

'Come with me. There's something I want to show you.'

Chapter 30

He pulls himself up from his seat using his forearms against the armrests, a manoeuvre that looks painful. His legs alone aren't strong enough. He walks towards the stairs and leads me to the first floor of the shop. There's a bedroom at the back. This must also be his home. The bedding is neatly pulled up. A pair of slippers are lined up on the floor and the curtains drawn back to reveal a leafy view from the back of the house. A tea cup rests on the bedside table next to a glasses case, a few books and a box of tissues. The side light has an old-fashioned lamp shade with tassels and the walls are covered in a lifeless pattern of greens and browns. Through a gap in the bathroom door, I can see a flannel draped over the sink and a cup holding a toothbrush and tube of toothpaste. I wonder if this is how the place looked when his wife was alive. I think about his lonely nighttime routine and the secrets he carries. He watches me as I scan the landing.

'Don't mind the mess,' he says, without turning to face me.

I nod, but he doesn't see. We walk to the front of the building into a room filled with paintings and more empty frames.

'These,' he says, breathing heavily, 'these are some of the paintings collected and those empty frames are the ones I still need to find.'

The air is thick with old resins. The curtains are drawn and the temperature is too cold for these works. I guess it's about fifteen degrees in here. The air is too dry. I recognise the paintings immediately: Picassos, Kandinskys, Kokoshkas, Matisses, Degas. It's a miniature art world of grand proportions in the upper room of a very ordinary shop in East Berlin. I turn to him and wait.

'What do you think?' he asks, and I wonder if he wants my opinion.

'These should be in a gallery,' I say and I can't believe the words coming out of my own mouth. I see signs of damage on a Matisse, leaning haplessly against more paintings whose identities are obscured by a Picasso. The way they are leaning against one other, open to damage, makes me wonder what he is doing.

'They are already damaged.' I say, brusquely. 'Who knows about them?'

'Only Maria, and now you,' he says, hesitantly. He lowers his head. 'I thought you might be able to help.'

'Help? How?'

'I wonder,' he says, hesitantly, 'whether you can help me find the owners? Maria tells me this is what you are doing.'

'Has she?' I feel exposed. 'And the empty frames?'

'Can you use your contacts to trace the ones that are lost? My sources tell me many have been sold on the black market for cash payments. Somebody who knows Schneider says that much of the work is being distributed through Vienna.'

'I can't promise anything. It's a huge operation and I'm working alone.'

He stares at me. 'You're smart and insightful. Don't waste your life following orders you don't want to take. I was in your shoes once and I regret some of the moves I made. Life is short. Don't let people make you do things you'll later regret.'

'We might as well go out and get some food.' I say.

He purses his lips, furrows his forehead, then he nods. 'Why not? I haven't been out for a meal in a long time. Even longer since I spent time with an interesting young girl.'

I feel more at ease with his forthrightness than I do with people tiptoeing around with words that don't mean anything. I don't take offence and he's right. I want to find out more about his past and the paintings. He seems to know far more about me than I do about him.

The image of my grandfather and my doll returns. This time, I hear Omama talking about my parents and I know that something bad has happened. I can smell the resin and the turpentine. The brushes have been thrown down on the floor in a rush and a half painted canvas of a still life sits fixed against the easel. The room is still. I hear the birds outside and a door closes abruptly somewhere in the distance. I'm alone in the room, sitting on the wood floor looking at the woollen hair on my doll and wanting to pull it out, to make her hairless. I want to see what she would look like if she lost her hair.

What did they go through? Their paintings and possessions taken, their freedom lost, their lives of no value? And here I am taking pieces for collectors and vast sums of money. Those families might even have owned some of the pieces, after losing their jobs, their homes, everything.

I remember the look on Schneider's face when he asked me what his brother was wearing and if there was a note. I realise, from Peter's words, that I've vastly underestimated Schneider. I think about the iron gate, the black bars curling and twisting, threatening to keep me trapped.

I remember Albert's apartment and the gunshot, the pipe on the mantelpiece. The smoking tip was orange with a deep curve. Opa had once told me they were porous, allowing you to smoke different blends without the taste being affected. A packet lay next to the pipe, deep blue with pale grey writing. I can smell the scent of burnt tobacco. I realise, now, that this was the same pack and the same pipe that I saw in Herr Schneider's apartment on the bookshelves, a classic Meerschaum pipe, its end carved as a fox running in circles, chasing its tail, trying to catch a moving target, never reaching the tip.

The letters from Albert were from Herr Schneider.

There is no Albert.

We reach Auguststrasse by tram. Peter points in the direction of the New Jewish Synagogue. 'The largest in Germany,' he says. 'My wife used to go before it was destroyed on Kristallnacht in 1938. Then it was bombed five years later. She never saw the new building, although I suspect she would have approved.' He points to the Kennedy Museum up the road. 'I remember exactly where I was when the news came in over the radio about his death ... Hitler.' He struggles to say the name. There are moments that you never forget – the scents, the sights, the sounds, where you were standing. You remember everything, the small details of your surroundings. The moment is fixed. 'I was standing here, waiting to meet him. Herr Schneider liked his food,' he says.

The Clärchens Ballhaus Café is on the corner of the street. It looks more French than German, an aroma of garlic and herbs drifting from the kitchen. The bar is stacked with bottles of red wine, liqueurs and an industrial coffee machine.

Peter hesitates before sitting down. He has decided against pulling out a chair for me. Maybe he thinks the age of chivalry has died. I don't mind either way. He has an unusual combination of grit and sensitivity. He feels familiar in some ways and the difference in our ages makes me feel comfortable around him.

'This is the last original surviving dance hall from the Weimar era.'

I try to imagine him dancing, swinging some young girl around the room. He looks as though he might have light feet. 'It's beautiful,' I say, 'comfortable, but grand. Did you dance?'

'Yes, but only with her. This was our last night out. Here. Before I lost her.' He pauses and rolls his eyes upwards, as though recalling a particular moment. 'She was a wonderful dancer.'

'I'm sure you weren't bad, either,' I say.

He smiles. 'Oh, the things that went on in this room. You young things think you're always the first. You wouldn't believe some of the sights. It was a riot. Tangos, live music and naughty cocktails were the order of the night. And then, who knew what would come next? Wonderful!'

'I'm sure.'

'You should see the ballroom upstairs. This is nothing in comparison. It has high ceilings, a chandelier, ornate moulding and candlelight.'

It's a world of dancing feet and light hearts, He gives me a look of pity. We both turn as the door opens. A man walks in and finds a table across from us. He faces me, pulls out a paper, orders a coffee without looking up.

'Peter, do you think Schneider's still moving paintings?'

'Yes, of course. It's not something you ever really retire from. I'm still trying to locate pieces. They don't come with a comfortable pension or a house in the mountains, unless you're lucky. You keep going.' I nod, thinking of what lies ahead for me. 'You think he's using you?' he asks.

'What makes you think that I know him?' I ask.

'The look in your eyes when I mentioned his name. You didn't need to say anything.'

We order meatballs with pepper cream, potatoes and broccoli, and two beers. The man with the paper watches while we're distracted with the menus. He gets up to leave and I feel uneasy as he passes me, the same as when the man in the train carriage flicked my lighter and when the letter was dropped onto my lap. Eyes, everywhere.

'I'll see what I can find out,' I say. 'Are the pieces catalogued?'

'Of course! I'll give you a copy.' There's relief in his eyes. 'So you will help? I would be really grateful.'

'I'll see what I can do but I can't promise anything.'

He tucks into the meat while I take a long sip of beer. 'Aren't you hungry?' he asks.

'I don't usually eat a large meal.'

'Eat up.'

I nod, then push a single meatball around the plate and stuff it into my mouth. It has soaked up the sauce and drips as it reaches my lips. He says nothing else until his plate is clean, eating as if starved.

'Peter, it will take some time. I'll have to search for gaps in the ownership histories of the pieces, and that means links with curators or breaking into files.'

He almost drains his beer and pauses, leaving a two finger measure at the bottom of the glass. 'I'd appreciate your help,' he says. 'There's a young man in Vienna. His name is Hans. I think he worked for The Art Loss Register in London.'

'Hans?' I freeze. How does he know Hans? What does

Hans have to do with this? 'Do you have a family name for him?' I try not to show any fear.

'No, just the first name. He trained in litigations somewhere and then helped track down stolen art. Much like you, but legitimate.' I no longer think Hans' work is legitimate, and I can't work out whether Knaus is impressed or repulsed by what I do. I can't ask him about Hans. Has he been tracking me? But if he had, I would have been arrested.

'Could there be one person holding all this work? A master collector?'

'Quite possibly,' he says, mopping the juice from his beard. 'But you'd have a hard job finding him.'

'Yes,' I say, wondering why he thinks that someone working on that scale would have to be male. I rest the cutlery to the side of the plate and order another beer. A spirit would be preferable, but this will do for now.

'Liesl, the Art Loss Register is made up mostly of art historians.'

'I know. I'm aware of their work,' I say.

'Hans was their in-house lawyer. He worked in their offices in Amsterdam and Cologne.' He pauses. 'There are insurance companies in London who hire people to find a piece and make a settlement before quietly putting it back out on the market. Don't underestimate him.'

'Do you think he's been following me? My apartment has been disturbed, files are missing, and I've had confrontations, shall we say?' Although no art went missing from my apartment.

'Quite possibly,' he says, without looking up.

'Do you have any more information? Peter, it's important.'

'No. Nothing,' he says, but I suspect he knows more. His head is down, foraging for every last morsel.

I try to imagine him shifting great works of art and networking with gallery owners and dealers. I'm probably underestimating him. I wonder if he has ever faced interrogation. I imagine that he wouldn't even flinch. His ability to remain calm is impressive. I expect it of myself, of course, but not others. I wonder about his conversations with Schneider, explicit or above board. I will never know.

Chapter 31

The train pulls into Westbahnhof station, the glow of lights
a welcome familiarity. People are moving from entrance to
platform, from platform to coffee shop, from coffee shop
towards home. Home is in a tall apartment in a Viennese
backstreet or an old building with a spiral, stone staircase
and curled railings with letter boxes stacked up and named
Lehmann, Burgermeier or Rothstein. I think of the
Meerschaum pipe, of the fox running in circles. There is no
Albert. It's me who has run in circles without catching a
tail. I think of all the visits to Schneider where I asked about
the Klimt sketches and waited for the next letter, and a clue
to help me unravel the mystery of the death of his brother.
Killed without remorse.

I remember the oil paints and blossom, sitting with my
doll, wondering what happened to Mama and Papa.

I reach my apartment, having taken a taxi from the station.
I couldn't face the trams and the waiting, not at this time
of night. Relief replaces the recent fear as I turn the key in
the lock. The few days in Berlin, and the meeting with Peter,
have been enlightening. I want to help him in some way, to
return the lost art. It will take more than one person, and
that's all I am, one pawn in a very large game. If there's no
Albert, and Herr Schneider is working for a Mr Big, as Peter
suggested, all the art is in one place and not distributed

amongst wealthy buyers, legitimate or otherwise. I think back to the first visit to Billrothstrasse where Schneider led me into his hallway and turned towards the kitchen, the stairs to my right leading to upstairs rooms, presumably empty, lined with more patterned wallpaper and heavy fabrics, a few ornaments and perhaps a bed. I pick up a bottle of vodka, but put it back, leaving the cigarettes lying next to the cabinet, and head towards my bedroom. My legs are heavy from the long journey. I sink into bed and pull the covers up around my neck, tight, leaving only space to breathe. A narrow shaft of moonlight catches the mirror on my wall, illuminating its ornate edging, a faux baroque piece I picked up in a flea market. It's worth nothing, except for its beauty. It's silver, not gold, as the original would be. I close my eyes and remember nothing more.

The next morning, I decide against meeting Maria, as arranged. Instead, I gather the papers, the brooch and the portrait painting from under the floorboards. I unroll it to look one last time. The colours are soft, blues and skin tones surrounding pink cheeks, eyes that look disappointed or embarrassed. There is a frizz of reddish hair, unkempt but striking. It's a Klimt, a rare beauty. I roll it up and put everything in the bag.

I down an espresso before leaving the apartment and wait until all footsteps below me fade. I close the main door of the building with a thud, a final closure before I dispose of the items in the bag. This will be the last time that I remain in possession of anything that does not belong to me. I get on the tram and head into the city centre. The leaves have turned without me noticing. I am always aware of the seasons and their changes, but not this time. Autumn has crept up on me as a thief in the night and will vanish without a trace, leaving the cool whites of winter snows, covering all traces of what once lay on the ground.

The tram judders and lurches. There's an empty seat, recently vacated, and I make my way towards it without damaging the contents of the bag. I watch the traffic and the lights as they change, from red to amber to green and back. All our lives are directed in some small way by signs, affected by changes in seasons, by people who come and go, as though we're on a fairground ride, endlessly turning, waiting for someone to step on or off. Some don't see it, missing the signs because they're too busy, too distracted, unable to trust their judgement, or maybe the signs are too small.

We stop on the east side of the ring and I walk the rest of the journey. I take my hat from a deep pocket and pull it down over my unruly curls until it won't spring back up. The walk is bracing and there are few people about, the tourists are gone now until next month when the markets start up again. It's hard to believe that a full year has passed since the last Christmas Markets.

I think back to being grabbed at the library and followed from the cathedral. I remember the outline of the person who watched me leave Albert's apartment, looking on as I dropped a glove and failed to go back to collect it, getting onto a tram instead and disappearing into the underground. And the toothbrush left lying on the floor in the apartment, the open window, the door lock not fully turned. I remember the warning in the letter and the fear that I should have felt, but didn't. The game has kept me on course, tied me to more letters and more dead drops. I reach the entrance of the police station and push through the doors. The desk is guarded by two police officers. One of them takes me through into a side room and turns on a tape after I tell him why I'm here. I put the bag down on a clinical table and he opens it. An onlooker might think that this meeting had been planned, that the police know why I'm here.

'Name,' he says, taking a pencil out and placing a form down on the table.

'Liesl Baumgartner, sir.'

He looks at me as if he knows me, then moves on. 'And the bag?'

'I want to hand these in.'

'These?'

'Yes,' I say, hoping I've made the right decision because you don't always know until after the event.

'And what are they?' he asks. He proceeds to pull everything out 'This looks as though it might be of value, if it's original,' he says, holding the brooch. I stay quiet. He unties the string on the canvas and unravels the painting. 'Would you mind explaining these to me and how they came into your possession?'

'The painting and the brooch I took. The papers are my own research, sir.'

'Are you trying to tell me you stole these items?'

'Yes. The brooch I took from a body on the street. The painting is from a gallery.'

He pulls out a pair of handcuffs before asking me again, 'Baumgartner, you said? Liesl?'

'Yes.' I have no idea how my name will change the consequences, but I want to step out of the circuit, the snare laid down by Schneider.

'Your parents' names?'

I haven't used their names since they were alive and, even

then, it was usually Mama and Papa. 'Florian and Anna, Sir. Why do you ask?'

He puts the handcuffs back through his belt. 'I was there the night of the crash. They were found dead on arrival. The car had rolled off the road and collided with a barrier. We looked for evidence of next of kin and found a photo of a girl in the woman's purse. I went with another officer to an address in the city. We found an elderly couple, a painter and his wife, with a young girl. Her name was Liesl.' I look down, hoping to hide my reaction. 'I thought I recognised your face when you walked in but it was so long ago.' I know how long ago it was, to the day, and how it feels even longer. I don't have anything to say to him. The room falls silent as he stops the tape. It clunks after a final whirr and everything is still.

'Officer, I just want to hand these things in. Please don't make me run through anything else.'

'If you can tell me why you took these or lead me to someone, we might be able to find a solution.' He stares at me as though he is still at the scene of the crash, as though he is fixed there, trying to work out how he might find that young girl. He won't expect to find her years later, a thief. He won't know how it will help her to stop spinning or prevent her from coming apart all together.

'I told you, I took them. The brooch I obtained from a body on the street at the top of the steps at Stephansplatz underground station. He was the brother of a Herr Schneider on Billrothstrasse. I can give you the address.' He starts up the tape again. 'I believe he killed him, sir, and sent me on operations around the city to collect art for various clients, although there were no clients. If you visit his home you may find everything tucked away there, undisturbed. And there is a Herr Knaus in Berlin who might be able to help you in your search.'

'Knaus.' He scribbles onto the form. 'Forename?'

'Peter. Peter Knaus.'

'The brooch looks like a Hapsburg brooch and the painting? Well, we'll have to get someone to evaluate it, but I suspect it might also be an original.'

I don't need experts to analyse these works, but why would he believe me? I have to remember that they're now in police custody and my hands and apartment are free of anything incriminating. I feel an unexpected sadness, a loss of not being able to unroll a painting and admire it over a late night drink. But I'm sure I've done something right, giving Maya Neumann back her grandmother's painting. I try to imagine how Peter would feel about my handing him in so quickly, but until everything is brought into the right hands, no loss can be properly restored.

'You know about the restitution laws?' he asks.

'Of course. I follow the art world and the legal aspects closely.'

'Then you'll know how significant this find will be for us and for the owners. If you're right.'

I nod and the meeting closes. The tape stops.

'Liesl, I should use this tape but it will incriminate you. If you can write down the Billrothstrasse address and the address in Berlin, I can let you go with no further questions.' He is risking his job. He hands me his pen and a piece of paper. I write down the details from memory and hand him the information with the knowledge that my parents' lives are an exchange for my release. He doesn't mention their names again. Instead, he thanks me with a look of understanding that I find almost alien, and shows me out of the room.

I exit the police station and head towards Stadtpark where I gave *Sundown* to Maya. I will no longer be able to contact her, or Maria or Hans. My life has to begin again, as though I never existed. I reach the park and find a bench. I sit and watch children running in circles through leaves that spiral from the trees, and I contemplate the idea of packing up my apartment and moving abroad. There won't be much to gather together, and the rental contract has a release clause, allowing me to terminate it without notice if I leave Austria.

A week passes between leaving the police station and sitting here, waiting for a flight out of Vienna to New York City. I pick up the paper I bought earlier this morning, without any cigarettes. The headline reads:

Europe's Largest Collection of Looted Art Found in the Vienna Home of One of the Most Prolific Hidden Collectors.

The subheading reads:

Link Found to Dealer in Berlin.

I scan the article and am relieved not to see my name. I've learned not to take what people say at face value. There are details of Schneider's arrest over the murder of his brother and images of the paintings stacked in what look like the upper rooms of this home. There's some information about his connections in Germany and an image of Peter Knaus. He looks peaceful. It would have been taken before they reached him. The journalist, a young man named Karl Goring, goes into detail about the links between the two, but I'm relieved to find out that Knaus has not been implicated, or arrested, and that he has agreed to help an organisation in Cologne with further restitution cases. I imagine he will feel a sense of relief that his life and his collection are no longer hidden and he has people to help return the works. I couldn't have fulfilled his wishes alone, but I'm glad we met. The memory of our meal in the café in Berlin will remain with me.

The sense of release comes as a surprise. I look across the aisle and watch a mother playing with her little girl. I'm grateful that Oma gave me the years she had left. It was enough to carry me through. I fold the paper and look out of the window, accepting a black coffee and a snack from the flight attendant. I have a job in New York as a gallery curator. It was found for me by some unknown source, but I know that Maria has contacts in the city. I believe she'll be relieved the truth is now public and she can move on. I'll send her a card from the gallery when my first day begins, a landscape or, more appropriately, a portrait of a girl, monochrome. On it, I will simply write the words, *Thank you, L.*

Acknowledgements

With enormous gratitude to my editor, Lynn Michell, whose keen eye for detail and passion for words has shaped this story into something better than I had anticipated. Her skill, intellect and thoughtfulness have been invaluable. She approached the manuscript with vigour and humour, making the task of editing much more pleasurable. Never have track changes been so entertaining! For believing in my writing and this story, thank you. To all at Linen Press, my heartfelt thanks for your time and energy in bringing this all together: to Bek, Rawaa, Kate, Laura and Ella.

My thanks go to the Dorotheum auction house, where a Canaletto painting with an estimated worth of ten million pounds sparked the beginnings of this story, and to ORF for organising Lange Nacht Der Musee (Long Night of Museums) in Vienna each year where the seeds were sown. To the Leopold, Albertina and Belvedere museums, for organising some wonderful art exhibitions. These have been inspirational and I have enjoyed many hours of wandering and observing varied styles of art in the most striking of settings.

During the eight years that I lived in the city, there were so many friendships that formed and have endured, leaving me with an ever-increasing love of the place. There are too many to name, but I want to thank Roswitha, Beata, Miri and fellow writer, Sylvia. Your friendship and support has been a valuable part of my journey. To the people of Vienna, those who have passed through and those who remain, viele Segnungen.

Sources

O'Donnell, T. 2011. 'The Restitution of Holocaust Looted Art and Transitional Justice: The Perfect Storm or the Raft of the Medusa?' European Journal of International Law, 22(1), 49–80.

'Art Restitution in Austria,' Federal Ministry, Republic of Austria: Arts and Culture. https://www.bmkoes.gv.at/en/Topics/arts-and-culture/culture/art-restitution-in-austria.html

'Arts Council Collection Loans Policy & Procedure.' https://artscouncilcollection.org.uk/sites/default/files/1_Loans_0.pdf

'Borrowing from the National Gallery: Loan Conditions (UK).' https://www.nationalgallery.org.uk/about-us/partnering-with-the-national-gallery/borrowing-from-the-national-gallery-a-guide?viewPage=2

'Entartete Kunst': The Nazis' inventory of 'degenerate art,' V&A Museum. https://www.vam.ac.uk/articles/entartete-kunst-the-nazis-inventory-of-degenerate-art

'Transnational Organized Crime.' Federal Bureau of Investigation. https://www.fbi.gov/investigate/organized-crime

Oskar Kokoschka, Guggenheim Collection Online. https://www.guggenheim.org/artwork/artist/oskar-kokoschka

Ingram Content Group UK Ltd.
Milton Keynes UK
UKHW020658200323
418838UK00015B/2217

9 781919 624860